D
Jm

D1561372

KEW FOR MURDER

A royal visit to the new computerised Public Record Office at Kew ends abruptly when, instead of the document she has requested to see, the system delivers a murdered body to the Princess. A trainee BBC producer is authorised to make a documentary of the police investigation of the murder. Then suspicion falls on certain researchers of the nation's archives, including the historian of the multinational Megalith Industries Ltd, who discovers a massive fraud perpetrated in World War II.

CHARLES CRUICKSHANK

KEW FOR MURDER

Complete and Unabridged

LINFORD
Leicester

First published in Great Britain by
Robert Hale Limited
London

First Linford Edition
published 2006
by arrangement with
Robert Hale Limited
London

British Library CIP Data

Cruickshank, Charles
    Kew for murder.—Large print ed.—
Linford mystery library
    1. Great Britain. Public Record Office—
Fiction 2. Murder—Investigation—England
—London—Fiction 3. Fraud—Fiction
    4. Documentary television programs—Fiction
    5. Detective and mystery stories
    6. Large type books
    I. Title
    823.9'14 [F]

    ISBN 1–84617–333–7

Published by
F. A. Thorpe (Publishing)
Anstey, Leicestershire

Set by Words & Graphics Ltd.
Anstey, Leicestershire
Printed and bound in Great Britain by
T. J. International Ltd., Padstow, Cornwall

This book is printed on acid-free paper

1

Although he did not know it — and it might have shaken even *his* boundless self-confidence if he *had* known it — Alistair Macalister's appointment as official historian to Megalith Industries Limited had been touch and go. The matter was finally resolved at one of the working lunches for which the firm is notorious.

Their dining-room occupies half the penthouse floor of the newest concrete and glass temple in the City — designed of malice aforethought to top by exactly one storey the forty-two of the National Westminster Bank building, formerly the tallest in Europe. The other half is devoted to the electronic kitchens, capable of producing a superb banquet for a hundred, but today ministering only to the midday needs of the twelve good men and true who direct the fortunes of MIL. A thousand feet below, strings of

1

barges moved up-river on the rippling blue afternoon tide, toys in the autumn sunshine. Along the pavements and across the miniature bridges innumerable City ants crawled, enjoying sixty minutes' respite from their task of invisibly supporting the nation's economy.

The smoked salmon, saddle of lamb and Stilton had been disposed of. MIL's twelve directors viewed each other complacently through a translucent haze of pleasantly scented cigar smoke. Now, over the port, a decision had to be made.

'Every other big firm has had its history written,' said the chairman, Sir Maurice Dyer, peevishly. 'Shell, BP, the lot. Why not us?'

He sipped his port and scowled at his deputy, Gilbert Archer, who had been against the project from the very beginning.

MIL's bicentenary was due in three years, an event which might well have passed unnoticed had not the chairman read history at Oxford. He was smitten with the idea that the firm should celebrate the event by publishing an account of its first two hundred years, and was already looking forward to sending complimentary copies suitably inscribed to large numbers of his friends.

'I just don't like the idea, Maurice,' said Archer. 'It's as simple as that.'

Because of the untimely death of the former chairman in a road accident nobody had been groomed for his job. Dyer had been brought in on his retirement from Whitehall as a permanent secretary, in preference to Archer, the heir apparent; and some colleagues suspected their occasional boardroom differences stemmed from this fact. Dyer was an impressive figure, six feet and broad in proportion. His massive bald dome hinted at considerable intellect. It also carried scars won as a front row forward in England's fifteen immediately after World War II — a qualification weighing heavily with some members of the board.

'I suppose Gilbert means there may be snags we're not likely to spot,' put in Sir Bernard Mitchell, responsible for MIL's engineering interests. Short and fat, with a walrus moustache that had earned him the inevitable nickname, he was an accountant by profession.

'Such as?'

'Libel, for one thing.'

'That *is* the danger,' agreed Archer.

Unlike the chairman he was almost invisible in a crowd. His thin face and sandy moustache enhanced his mouselike appearance, but on close acquaintance he revealed a dynamism hardly to be associated with the genus *Mus musculum*. He had won a hockey Blue in his university days; and his meteoric progress within MIL suggested that that game of skill might be better preparation for a career in industry than the front row of the scrum. Lesser men would have been upset when an outsider was brought in over their head. Archer accepted the decision without protest; but then he was ten years younger than Dyer. Sooner or later his turn would come.

These three — Dyer, Archer and Mitchell — formed an inner cabinet which thrashed out major issues and presented decisions to the full board almost as accomplished facts; but although the matter under discussion — the firm's history — was anything but major, the inner cabinet had failed to agree on it. It was a boardroom joke that whereas the biggest single order chased by the firm — a thousand-million-pound contract to supply missiles to the Ministry of Defence on which many pundits thought the survival of the MIL empire might depend — had gone through the inner cabinet almost on the nod, they had spent weeks arguing the toss about the history project without getting anywhere.

Most of the other board members were lukewarm. If the chairman wanted a toy to play with, what harm? Archer alone was strongly against.

'Call it instinct,' he said. 'I may be in a minority, but I'm still unhappy.'

'You *are* in a minority, Gilbert,' said Dyer, quick to seize on the admission. 'And we must settle this today. Chap's downstairs waiting to hear our decision.'

Reluctant to concede defeat, the deputy chairman said:

'There's no mileage these days in honest truth. All people are interested in is *dirt*. It sells better.'

'If we give him a generous fee,' replied Dyer, 'sales won't matter — and we'll get the unvarnished truth.'

'It's to be warts and all, then?' asked one of the younger directors.

'Any scholar worth his salt would insist on that.'

'*Is* he worth his salt?' demanded Archer. 'I've heard some pretty acid comment from some of his confrères.'

'So have I,' said the younger director. 'They say he's quite competent, but always has an eye to the main chance.'

'Don't we all,' observed Mitchell.

'Not your honest scholar.'

'It's all professional jealousy, I expect,' said Dyer. 'If we don't like the book we needn't publish it.'

'That'll put the cat among the pigeons all right,' said Archer. 'Think what the gossip columnists will make of it! 'MIL suppress skeleton in cupboard'. 'Mystery of the Missing History'.'

'You wouldn't make a fortune as a sub-editor, Gilbert,' said Mitchell.

Archer laughed. He reflected for a

6

moment and then went on:

'It isn't the greatest issue of all time. We can't discuss it for ever. I agree — with reluctance. Go ahead.'

There was a thankful murmur of support round the table.

'Like to join me when I see him?' asked Dyer.

'Your baby,' said Archer shortly. 'Happy to leave him in your arms. Hope he doesn't wet you too much.'

★ ★ ★

Alistair Macalister was in fact still something of a baby. Pink-complexioned, in his early thirties, already tending to a donnish plumpness from too hearty patronage of Balliol's well-stocked High Table. A mass of waving golden hair fell over his shoulders in the modern fashion which even his sponsor Dyer found slightly revolting. Equally unpleasant was his habit of flashing an ingratiating and patently insincere smile, especially when the conversation took a difficult turn.

His father had been — still was — a

great friend but it was suddenly born in upon Dyer that the adage 'Like father, like son' was not a universal truth. It was several years since he'd met the son, in fact the boy had just left public school, and he had grown from a pleasant youth into, Dyer was forced to admit, a thoroughly unpleasant young man. He was alarmed to find himself having second thoughts. Had he been wrong to bulldoze his colleagues into accepting his nominee? Was there, as Archer had suggested, a hidden pitfall which he had not foreseen? However, he'd crossed his Rubicon. There was no turning back.

'You appreciate, of course, that we must reserve the right to delete any passages in your book we consider — ah — inappropriate? Naturally, without prejudice to your fee?'

'It might prejudice my reputation,' responded Macalister quickly. Then, seeing the other did not like this very much, flashed his smile and said: 'I'm sure we'll have no problems on that score.'

Dyer was visibly relieved. He said:

'Excellent! Now, how d'ye propose to tackle the assignment?'

'The firm's papers are in first-class order, especially the material covering your early years in Birmingham. Miss Warner is to be congratulated.'

Penelope Warner was the firm's archivist, responsible for the custody of their records which stretched back two centuries to the formation of the original small engineering works in the Midlands, from which the MIL empire was descended.

'She'll be delighted to hear it.'

'And of course your World War II records. Taken together with the Government papers — '

'Government papers?' Dyer broke in in astonishment.

Macalister looked equally surprised.

'Yes. In the war years you and your subsidiaries were for all practical purposes a Government agency. Without drawing on the official papers I'd be telling only half the story.'

'Yes, yes. I recognize that, but — '

'I sometimes think the writing of history is a sort of chemical reaction,' said

9

Macalister, embarking on a proposition which all his undergraduate pupils had had to endure at one time or another. 'You may remember that sulphur and potassium sulphate are pretty innocuous in themselves. Mix 'em together and hit 'em with a hammer and you get an almighty bang. We used to frighten the wits out of our chemistry master.'

Macalister smiled at the recollection. Yes, said Dyer to himself. I can see you would have enjoyed that. The historian went on:

'If you take two sets of records dealing with the same subject, perhaps neither very interesting in its own right — two sets of half truth, as it were — they're your chemicals. Mix 'em — '

'To get an atomic explosion?'

'Happily nothing so violent,' replied Macalister, smiling and running his hand affectionately through his golden locks. 'But it's the only way to arrive at the whole truth — mighty above all things.'

'Apocrypha,' the chairman murmured absently. He had been brought up on the Bible. 'Esdras, Book One, Chapter iv.'

He was still weighing the implications of this development. The idea that their historian should delve into official files was somehow disturbing — one that hadn't occurred to him when he was pressing for the history to be written, but certainly one he should have thought of. He felt that it might prove troublesome; but he could hardly go back to his colleagues now. Aloud he said:

'I read history at Balliol, as I expect you know, and I should have realized you would want to go wider than just our own records. There's two centuries' worth of them and we had assumed they'd be enough. However, I see your point,' the chairman concluded reluctantly.

'I don't anticipate any difficulty,' said Macalister summoning up yet another smile.

'What programme d'ye have in mind? What timetable?'

'I insist on precise deadlines,' replied the historian. 'One of my weaknesses. I've no time for people, retired ambassadors in particular, who try to write their memories in the intervals of the social round, pruning the roses, playing golf or whatever, and seldom get beyond Chapter One. They don't realize that writing one's life is more of a full-time job than living it — there's so much less time for it. Perhaps it's just as well they *don't* get past Chapter One. I'll deliver the typescript to you two years from the date of my contract. Not a day sooner, not a day later. You'll neither hear nor see me again for twenty-four months.'

The rest of the conversation was devoted to the nuts and bolts of Macalister's contract. When he had departed, Dyer found himself in a state of considerable irritation, partly because he had authorized the historian to draw on official papers concerned with the firm's affairs — to mix what Macalister called two sets of half truth in the interests of finding the whole truth — without getting the specific approval of his board; and more particularly because he had already embarked on his own autobiography, of which he had not completed even Chapter One. Indeed, little more than the possible titles — *Personal File: thirty years in Whitehall*, or perhaps better, *Memoirs of a Mandarin* — had been committed to paper.

He consoled himself with the thought that it would be two years — no more, no less — before the vexed question of the firm's history need reappear on the board's agenda.

★　★　★

His cronies at the village club pulled Michael Carrington's leg unmercifully when they became aware of his proposed enterprise. Nothing was more out of character than that he should write a book — and a scholarly book at that. It is true that the subject he had chosen — gambling — seemed to be right up his street, for he was a loyal supporter of the village betting shop, but when they knew that he intended to study *Gambling in the reign of Elizabeth I* most of his fellow club members were left speechless with astonishment.

Just what Carrington's antecedents were no one knew for certain. Election to the village club was rather easier than to the Reform or the Athenaeum. No elaborate curriculum vitae supported by a dozen signatures was called for. It was enough if the candidate had stood a member of the committee a pint at the *Amazon and Tiger*. It was known that he had been in the SAS for a spell immediately after World War II. Then his career became obscure. He allowed it to be believed he had served in the Foreign and Commonwealth Office; and the total absence from his make-up of the airs and graces usually associated with a diplomat suggested a backroom assignment in that distinguished Department of State. But whether this meant he had been a registry clerk concerned with the handling of files, or, at the other end of the backroom scale, a secret agent, the village club could not make up its mind.

His friend Bodley had gone out of his way to solve the problem by consulting *Who's Who* in the local library, without avail. Carrington, Michael, did not feature in that massive record of the country's great and good; and it was impossible to decide whether the omission was because his job had been too insignificant or too secret. The more reticent he was about his career the more his friends built it up, such is the perversity of human nature. There were a dozen explanations of the scar on his right forehead, each more exciting than the last. His very slight limp was variously attributed to an awkward parachute landing in the Malayan emergency, to having had his foot crushed by a half-track during an exercise in arctic Norway, and to a Russian bullet while he made a hair's-breadth escape from the Hungarian uprising. No one would have accepted for a moment that it was due to an incipient arthritic hip.

He enjoyed unashamedly the awe in which he was held by his fellow members, and was accustomed to hold court in the club every Saturday evening. He had an inexhaustible fund of stories covering the whole spectrum from purest white to darkest blue. There was no topic to which he did not automatically react, like a Pavlovian dog answering its dinner bell.

Bodley, whose own career was an open book — forty years in a local solicitor's office without being offered a partnership — deemed Carrington's scholarly ambition a foolish aberration. He said:

'You're not cut out for this sort of thing, old man. Even if you do write a book, you'll never find a publisher in these times. Especially for a subject like that.'

The two men could hardly have been more different. Carrington, the rugged man of action, whose charm got him his own way most of the time, but who left the impression that he would not hesitate to use less pleasant means when charm failed. Just turned 50, with a mass of curly black hair just beginning to grey at the sides, and piercing blue-grey eyes constantly probing and assessing, a characteristic some attributed to his presumed late profession.

Bodley, also a bachelor, was very much the product of his career. Precise, methodical, careful to think before committing himself. Secretly anxious to make his mark but never having the courage to step outside his natural self. It would be too much to say he hero-worshipped Carrington but he had at times imagined himself playing Bunny to Raffles/Carrington, but in something more exciting than writing a book.

'I've got to do something, Bodley, or I'll go round the bend. I simply can't be a contented cabbage like you and the other chaps here.'

He indicated the evening drinkers of the village club with an all-embracing sweep of his pewter tankard. Bodley found himself beginning to understand. He himself had taken to retirement as a duck takes to water, perhaps because he had never been under pressure in his job. After thirty years as a secret agent (if he *had* been a secret agent) Carrington must have found it a shock to be put out to grass. The public servant is tossed on the scrap heap punctually on his or her sixtieth birthday. The permanent secretary picks up a few directorships. The clerk is hired to keep books in his suburb. But the secret agent does not exist. He cannot be provided with a testimonial enumerating the highlights and successes of his career.

'Further,' Carrington went on, 'I'm not particularly interested in having my book published. I'll be seeking truth for its own sake, indulging in scholarship which is its own reward,' he concluded pompously.

'Poppycock,' said Bodley. 'I suppose it's an obsession and there's no point in arguing with the obsessed. I only hope you'll see reason before it's too late.'

'You should try it yourself, old man.'

'Thanks very much,' replied Bodley. 'What with my allotment, and meals on wheels, I've got enough on my plate as it is. I haven't even time to keep a diary.'

Curiously enough, when Carrington defended his project he seemed singularly knowledgeable on the subject. He planned to study the relationship between gambling and the decline of archery in the sixteenth century when men who should have been practising with the long bow, so that they might defend their country against the Spaniards, were enjoying themselves in illegal gaming houses. He even quoted Roger Ascham at his friends: archery helped bodily health, quickness of wit and the defence of the realm. Gambling led to loss of reputation, loss of goods and the winning of gout and dropsy. The consensus of opinion was that Carrington must be slightly off his rocker, but it was a free country. If he wanted to follow in the steps of Gibbon, no one was going to stop him. None of them need buy his book, in the unlikely event that it would ever see the light of day.

★　★　★

When Maurice Dyer joined MIL he sold his modest Kensington home and moved into the ten-bedroom mansion at Cobham which the firm provided for the chairman. The spacious grounds and large public rooms were ideal for entertaining, a pastime at which Dyer excelled. The MIL garden party during Wimbledon fortnight was one of the events of the season — which the chairman's wife could have done without. She hated parties and contrived to spend much time behind the scenes, pretending to look after the reserves of drinks and short eats, but actually to avoid having to meet her guests face to face. She reminded her husband of a schoolboy seemingly trying desperately to reach the fiercest action of a rugger game, but always failing to get there by the narrowest of margins.

When he told her she would have to play hostess at a party unscheduled in the MIL calendar — to launch the firm's history project — she had the temerity to question the need for the event. Dyer was furious that the boardroom opposition to his pet scheme should have spread to his home.

'This book is important, Matilda,' he said angrily. '*Very* important. It must be given every chance. When it does come out those who are against it now will be the first to take the credit.'

'So somebody's against it. Who?'

'The entire board, if you must know. Can't think why. It's a perfectly normal thing for a firm like us. We've got a first-rate Oxford don to write it — Buster

Macalister's son. You remember Buster? Anyhow, all you need worry about is organizing the party. Which I'm sure you'll do very well. We want to get off on the right foot.'

Lady Dyer sighed. Sooner or later Maurice would have to retire from this job too, and the placid twilight years to which she had looked forward for so long would at last be within her grasp.

★   ★   ★

'Good God!'

Gilbert Archer could not believe his eyes.

'Trouble?' asked Bernard Mitchell, who was in Archer's office.

'I can't believe it. Maurice has done some bloody silly things in his time, but this takes the cake!'

He thrust the guest list for the party to launch the firm's history into Mitchell's hand, pointing to a name near the bottom.

'Julian Hardcastle?' said Mitchell. 'Never heard of him.'

'Philistine,' observed Archer. 'As a matter of fact he's the chap I'd have chosen to write our history, if it *had* to be written, instead of Maurice's nepotistic Macalister.'

'Nepotistic?'

'He's the son of Buster Macalister. They were up at Oxford together — Maurice and Buster, that is. Maurice wanted to keep it dark from the board — in case it influenced their decision.'

'To stop us knowing it was jobs for the boys? Well, well!'

'Now Dyer asks Hardcastle to meet the man who was handed the job on a plate. I ask you!'

'Will he come?'

'I certainly shouldn't in the circumstances,' said Archer. 'Unless to stick a knife in Macalister.'

The party followed the usual course for such events. The more important guests adroitly disengaged themselves from the less important so that they might talk business among themselves. The less important coalesced round the cold buffet where they made short work of the caviar and canapés. Those of the literary editors of the national newspapers and learned journals who had deigned to turn up amused themselves lacerating the reputations of the latest best-selling novelists. The ebb and flow round the room gradually washed the women to one end where they could find sanctuary from business discussions. The noise level steadily increased until it was impossible to hear a word spoken by anybody — immaterial since by this time most people were interested only in what they themselves were saying.

The contretemps came just as Sir Maurice Dyer had decided the psychological moment had arrived and was about to call Macalister to the end of the room to introduce him to the company and say a few words about the proposed history. The chairman was horrified to see the guest of honour confronted by a very large bald-headed man who had clearly visited the bar once too often. It was obvious that they were not engaged in friendly conversation.

Before their host or anyone else would reach them, Hardcastle had grasped the lapels of Macalister's jacket and was shaking him violently, as an outsize terrier might shake an outsize rat. At the same time he was addressing him in language hardly suitable for a polite cocktail party. He suddenly released him and, while the golden-haired young man was still off balance, thumped him squarely on the jaw. The blow precipitated Macalister backwards into an oasis of potted palms hired for the occasion. Shattered palm fronds, fragments of flowerpots, several pounds of earth, and MIL's historian fell in an untidy heap.

One or two guests made it their business to restrain the assailant. Others hastened to disentangle the victim from the debris. The party began to disperse at record speed. Hardcastle slunk away shamefacedly. Macalister, when he had dusted the earth from his trousers, made an equally swift departure, having mumbled his thanks to host and hostess through a split lip. The literary editors were delighted. Here at least was something their gossip columnist colleagues could make good use of. The chairman's carefully prepared words apropos of the firm's history were left unuttered.

'What on earth was that in aid of?' he demanded when the last guest had gone.

Archer was still angry with him for setting the scene for the unpleasantness. He replied:

'Professional jealousy, aided and abetted by your bloody silly guest list. And too many Scotches. I guess Hardcastle thought he'd been invited to give Macalister the chance to crow over him. I guess Macalister *did* crow over him and got what he deserved. Hardcastle used to be quite a useful boxer, and he's still in good shape.'

'Well, I'm damned!' said Dyer. 'I thought the two would have something in common, and Hardcastle might be willing to give Macalister a helping hand.'

'Helping fist, more like,' observed Archer grimly. 'I wish to God we'd never gone ahead with this business.'

'Come off it, Gilbert. A punch-up isn't the end of the world.'

'There'll be other punch-ups,' replied the deputy chairman gloomily. 'Mark my words.'

2

In spite of Gilbert Archer's prognostication the path of scholarship ran smooth for the next three months. With the reluctant blessing of his college Alistair Macalister rearranged his schedule of lectures and tutorials in Oxford to allow him to spend a good deal of time in London, where he had taken a bed-sitter in Bloomsbury conveniently situated near the British Library, and from which he could easily get to the Public Record Office at Kew.

Hardcastle was also working in the PRO, and although the pair occasionally came perilously near rubbing shoulders, for example, when collecting their documents from the Distribution Counter, or in the cafeteria queue, there was no further punch-up. They were watched with interest by the regular readers some of whom hoped that open warfare would continue, but they were disappointed.

At the opposite end of the scholarship scale Michael Carrington continued to work on his monograph on gambling in the sixteenth century. In spite of Richard Bodley's earlier refusal to have anything to do with Carrington's book, he was now formally acting as his research assistant, thanks to a curious chain of events that began one evening in the village club.

'This book of mine,' Carrington had said, after threading his way back from the bar without spilling a drop of Whitbread, 'is more difficult that I thought. It's really a two-man job. Cheers!'

'Cheers!' responded Bodley. Then, feeling that some comment was required, added: 'A two-man job? So what?'

'That's where you come in, Dick.'

'Me?' said Bodley in some amazement.

'The second man.'

'Like hell! From what you've been saying — '

He had to admit he was not quite sure what Carrington had been saying. When his friend was in full flight on a Saturday evening he was accustomed to let his mind wander, not because he disapproved of Carrington's performance as a raconteur, even when he sank to fourth-form level, but because there were other matters more worthy of his attention — would *Match of the Day* live up to expectations, or would the new putting gimmick suggested by the assistant professional really pay off?

'If only you would listen,' said Carrington severely, 'you would realize that not only is literature fun, it can be profitable.'

'Some hope,' said Bodley cynically.

'However, as I say I need help. I'm offering you the post of research assistant. Paid, of course.'

'How much?'

'Fifty pounds a week.'

'You must be joking!'

'If you saw the load of files I've to go through you'd see what I mean. Forget your fellow vegetables, and give me a hand.'

Bodley resented being equated with the score of elderly gentlemen steadily working their way through their Saturday evening liquid ration. Discussing local scandal, appraising yesterday's telly, recounting for the twentieth time anecdotes that were fresh only because the listeners had forgotten they'd heard them nineteen times before. Of course, he was different, a cut above the others, with interests stretching far beyond the confines of the village club. Maybe difficult to say on the spur of the moment just what they were, but . . . Oh, hell! Why not admit it? Carrington could be right.

'Then it's settled?' said his friend, seeming to read his mind.

'No, it's not,' said Bodley suddenly. 'Forget the whole thing.'

The following Saturday Carrington resumed his attack. With no more success.

'Vegetable I may be,' said Bodley, 'but I'm a contented vegetable. There must be masses of people who could help you. Graduates looking for a job. Retired people on a low pension. Why not advertise?'

'I need somebody I know. Somebody I can get on with. Somebody I can *trust*.'

Bodley was touched and almost won over. He said:

'Sorry, Mike. It's not my cup of tea.'

Later that evening his first sensation as he pushed open the front door of No. 14 Attlee Close was the amused self-pity with which the elderly regard themselves when they do something particularly stupid. He was about to enter the wrong house.

Amusement gave way to horror. It was the right house but it had been transformed. The hall had been stripped. The Queen Anne chest of drawers, the Chippendale chair, his grandmother's mahogany wall mirror — all had gone. Their total absence was emphasized by the bare uneven floorboards no longer masked by the rich Turkey carpet. There was worse to follow. The perfect set of eight Sheraton chairs, inherited from an aunt and totally out of place in his tiny dining-room, had followed the contents of the hall; and with them had gone a sizeable part of Bodley's material wealth. Every room had been emptied. The only movable not removed was the telephone, sitting in splendid isolation on the naked living-room floor.

It was not the empty house, shattering though it was, that knocked the bottom out of Bodley's world. It was the awful recollection of a letter that came two days ago. A courteous reminder that the premium on his insurance policy, which laid the responsibility for the contents of his house on the broad shoulders of the Great Southern Assurance Company, was one month overdue. Until such time as the company received his cheque, Bodley's frail shoulders must carry the burden unaided.

The lawyer in him had been horrified by his carelessness, and he had resolved to deal with the letter immediately after breakfast. However, a fault in his electric toaster had filled the kitchen with acrid smoke and threatened to set the place on fire. Instead of confirming the importance of sending an instant reply to the Great Southern, as might have been expected, this event had driven the matter of insurance from his head — to which it was now forcibly returned.

At least he could call the police.

The sergeant who sleepily answered the phone was torn between sympathy for the victim and admiration for the thieves.

'Brilliant, sir! You've got to hand it to them. Third time this month — in the county that is. Steal a van, clear the house as clean as a whistle, and away they go. Probably got a cuppa from your neighbours.'

'Could it be a mistake?'

'Like demolishing the wrong building?' The sergeant was amused. 'Wouldn't bet on it. But there's always the insurance. Constable Sanders is on the way, sir.'

The constable echoed the sergeant's admiration.

'Professional,' he said approvingly. 'Cool customers, all right. Must 'ave known you'd be away. Are your movements regular?'

He decided that his choice of words was infelicitous.

'I mean, are you at business all day. Leaving the house empty?'

'I'm a bachelor,' replied Bodley. 'I leave most days about ten, either to go to the village club or the golf club. I don't get back till after six. Later on a Saturday.'

'Regular 'abits is a gift to the criminal classes,' said the constable with satisfaction. 'That's how diplomats get theirselves kidnapped — '

'I'm not a diplomat,' interrupted Bodley irritably, 'and I haven't been kidnapped — '

'No need to go off at the deep end, sir.'

With that Constable Sanders adjourned to interview the neighbours. Their disgruntled evidence, most of them having gone to bed, amounted to little. A furniture van in the red and yellow livery of Rembrandt Removals had drawn up at ten o'clock. No one had paid much attention. One or two were surprised that Mr Bodley was leaving the district without announcing the fact; but then he kept himself to himself.

The four men had not been given cups of tea but they did exchange cordial words with one neighbour as they were leaving. Well spoken, English judging by their accents. This man had been surprised by their energy. 'First-class types — really seemed to enjoy their work.'

'I'll bet,' said Bodley gloomily when the constable reported this assessment.

When he was alone again the disconsolate householder squatted on the bare boards where he might now be watching *Match of the Day*, with a generous nightcap by his side. He dialled Carrington's number. When he heard his voice he announced without any preliminaries:

'I'll take that job — if it's still open.'

There was an exultant cheer at the other end of the line. Bodley continued:

'Meantime, can you lend me a camp-bed?'

'What on earth for?'

'Yes or no?'

'There's a safari bed somewhere around, I think.'

'And blankets?'

'Yes, yes. Are you off on a camping expedition?'

'I've been burgled. Comprehensively. Every bloody stick.'

'Good Lord!'

Carrington sounded genuinely sympathetic.

'That's only half of it. You remember I told you a couple of days ago I was being dunned by my insurance company?'

'Yes?'

'Well, I never sent them a cheque — which is why I need your job.'

'Well, I'm damned!' said Carrington. 'It's an ill wind, I suppose — I'll get Mrs Hoskins to look out the camp-bed and things — unless you'd rather doss down here?'

'No thanks. I'll be round in twenty minutes. At least they didn't take my car.'

So it was that Richard Bodley found himself acting as Carrington's dogsbody in the pursuit of knowledge in the Public Record Office at Kew. His job was to locate the documents which threw light on Carrington's chosen subject and then pass them on to his friend for further study. At first he had great difficulty in finding his way through the hundreds of Lists and Indexes — the massive tomes which led researchers to the documents they wanted — but he struck up a friendship with an elderly spinster, Miss Ernestine Dudley, who took pity on him when she saw him floundering. She said she was a record agent, one of a group who made their living searching the records on behalf of people, usually Americans, and usually trying to trace their British ancestors, who could not themselves come to the Record Office.

She became so motherly so quickly that Bodley began to suspect she had designs on him, in spite of his professed poverty (he had told her about the misfortune which brought him to Kew); but he was nevertheless grateful for her help without which he would have found the going hard.

He devilled assiduously for two weeks, discovering much that was entertaining in the files of the first Elizabeth, quite apart from the gambling which was his main task; and he had no doubt he was making a useful contribution to Carrington's book.

Then the blow fell. A somewhat sheepish Carrington — most unlike his usual self — accosted him early one evening in the village club.

'I say, old man. I'm not sure how to put it, but I've come to the conclusion that — '

He paused, and Bodley, sensing the worst, finished the sentence for him.

'You don't need my services any longer?'

'I'm terribly sorry, but — '

'My work hasn't come up to scratch?'

'Of course it's not that. I've no doubt you've a flair for research. Fact is, I've had one or two knocks on the stock market . . . '

'Not to worry,' said Bodley wearily, accepting defeat. 'I'll get by. Won't be easy, but if I give up this place, *and* the golf club . . . '

'I *am* sorry,' repeated Carrington. 'Devilish sorry.' He sounded as if he meant it.

It was left at that. However, Bodley simply didn't believe the story about the stock market. Something else had happened to make his friend declare him redundant. He was sure it couldn't be the quality of his work — he had done everything that had been asked of him and a bit more besides. He'd no doubt about *that*. But what could have gone wrong?

For the next few days he was too busy assessing whether he could afford to keep on No. 14 Attlee Close to speculate about Carrington's somersault. The generous salary he'd offered would have made all the difference to his finances; but there it was. He must now rely on his own meagre resources. Which meant resigning from the golf club, and the more modest village club, and selling his car.

This enabled him to refurnish his home, but on a scale which a Victorian workhouse would have been ashamed of. It also left him with empty days and empty evenings with only the disc jockeys of Radio 2 for company. It had been impossible to replace his beloved Sony TV. At first he sought refuge in the village library, sharing tables with senior citizens in like case, reading newspapers and tattered magazines in which he had little interest. He was beginning to wonder how long he could endure this existence when it occurred to him that not only was the Public Record Office free, comfortable, and admirably furnished — certainly a cut above the village library — but people like his new friend Ernestine Dudley were actually able to make a living there, or so it seemed. He could get to Kew inexpensively by means of the bicycle which had replaced his car, and also easily since the seven-mile run was flat most of the way. A much more healthful means of transport as he frequently told himself when battling against a headwind in a rainstorm.

Miss Dudley warned him it might be some time before any business came his way, but promised to hand on any enquiries she was too busy to handle herself, and to encourage her fellow record agents to do the same. In the meantime she suggested he should pass the time by doing some research on his own account, to familiarize himself with the ways of the office. He settled down happily to studying the history of colonial Malta, partly because he had once spent an enjoyable holiday in that island,

and partly because of a poster in Kew Gardens Station advertising the twentieth-century delights of the place.

The police had made no headway in tracking down his stolen furniture, although they had got some help from a minor informer which led them to believe that his precious antiques, together with the others stolen in the county by the same gang, had found their way abroad either to the Continent or to America. They had also a suspicion that the self-appointed removal men had been tipped off that No. 14 Attlee Close would be unoccupied by someone in the village, but whether he was a resident or someone sent in to spy out the land they could not say. All this was cold comfort.

3

Peter Plumb, a very junior member of the Science and Features Department of BBC TV, recently down from Oxford, fresh-faced and fresh-minded, was mildly puzzled.

As he crunched through the frozen snow between Kew Gardens Station and the Public Record Office the scene had been exactly as it should be on this last Thursday in December. The customary trickle of dedicated newsmen and news-women bent on exercising their peculiar *ius primae noctis* — the annual licence to the Press to view public documents newly released under the 'thirty-year rule' before they were made available to legitimate scholars. Heads down against the biting north wind, they hurried miserably along Burlington Avenue praying to find a sensational headline in the lucky dip — some hitherto unsuspected indiscretion of the Prime Minister of thirty years ago, more likely an addle-pated memorandum by the Foreign Office of the day, or — too good to be true — a revealing letter from the Head of the Secret Intelligence Service signed with the purple ink 'M' which is his prerogative, and intended to be secret until doomsday and beyond.

All this was common form. His colleagues had warned Peter about the annual journalistic jamboree. What came as a surprise was the frenzied activity around the great space-age building recently erected by the taxpayer to house the nation's records, and nicknamed 'Fort Ruskin' from the street at the end of which it stood.

Strange vehicles in the large car-park and outside the main entrance. In spite of the weather the broad steps were being scrubbed until the Aberdeen granite sparkled in the pale winter sunshine like a *diamanté* collar. In the more tolerable temperature within, air-conditioned to preserve alike Magna Carta and less memorable latter-day minutes, a squad from the Department of the Environment was vacuuming the blue Axminster carpet in the spacious entrance hall, making a row like a flight of Concordes. The hall itself, a barren desert when Peter had left late on the previous evening, was a luxuriant green oasis teeming with well-nourished wandering Jews, Swiss cheese plants and spike-leaved spiders.

It was left to the omniscient *Times*, a tall elegant young man with the profile of a Greek god, whom Peter knew slightly, to explain the mystery. As they checked in their overcoats and briefcases he shouted over the uproar:

'Royal visit!'

Having imparted this information *The Times* strode masterfully upstairs to the Reading Room, two steps at a time, not a moment to be lost in the fight for open government, or the search for a juicy scoop. As an afterthought he called over his shoulder:

'Why the hell have Them and Us on the same day?'

The question had earlier worried the management of the Public Record Office. To deny the Press first whack at the cream of the nation's indiscretions of thirty years ago, due to be released to the public at large on the second of January, in the interests of a royal visit would produce a concerted howl from Fleet Street. It would be seen as a deliberate attack on the freedom of the Press, if not actually an attempt to introduce a police state.

On the other hand, a royal command — even a minor one — could not be ignored. However, it was suggested that if the visit were made very informal, both First and Fourth Estates could be accommodated at the same time. And so, with the approval of the Lord Chancellor, the minister responsible for the safe keeping of the public records, it had been decided.

In the Reading Room on the first floor the signs of unwonted activity were equally evident. Ultra-modern canvasses by famous artists — mainly of the surrealist poached-egg genre — had been hastily rawlplugged to the bare concrete walls. The Lists and Indexes on the lengthy shelves of the adjoining Reference

Room had been dusted and replaced, their spines aligned with the precision of a Guards' battalion on parade. The only hint of disorder was at the far end of the Reading Room where the corralled Press were already thumbing their way through the newly released files, scribbling in shorthand books and muttering feverishly into tape recorders. The great annual dirt race was well under way.

Peter Plumb was not a competitor. He was engaged in a comparatively innocent enterprise — research for a TV series on famous shipwrecks based on old Admiralty papers and inevitably starting with Henry VIII's *Mary Rose*. Still imbued with virtuous scholarly ideals he viewed with distaste the assembled Press persons and speculated as to how many unnecessary accounts of non-events of thirty years ago would lead off in tomorrow's front pages with the formula: 'Today it is revealed that . . . '

For the Record Office staff the preceding week had been a double nightmare. The rank and file had the impossible task of locating all the papers the Press were likely to call for — if any were not produced instantly the headlines would certainly shout 'Government Attempt Cover-up!' The senior officers had worked equally hard organizing a tour to do justice to the office without interfering too much with the activities of ordinary readers.

A handful of citizens of Kew, diverted from their shopping round by an announcement in the stop press of the *Kew Advertiser* (a journal more interested in last week's weddings than the shady events of thirty years ago) that the Princess was due to visit them, were at last rewarded by the arrival of the royal cavalcade. Two limousines, the first with the Princess and a lady in waiting, the second with her private secretary and detective.

The party was welcomed by the Lord Chancellor, and after a brief pause for the benefit of an Independent Television News crew, cursing the schedule that brought them to the arctic wastes of Kew, disappeared inside.

'Luvly, ain't she?' said one of the

shivering matrons. 'Looked me straight in the eye. Maybe I'll be on the telly tonight.'

The show over, she and her companions drifted away towards Ruskin Avenue, stamping their frozen feet, to resume their daily round.

★   ★   ★

An hour earlier Ernest Pepperbred, assistant keeper, Administration, had exchanged his business suit for a morning coat (courtesy Moss Bros.) behind a locked office door to avoid an embarrassing confrontation with his secretary. He had been told to explain the computerized system of document retrieval to the royal guest and guide her hand when she asked the computer to produce a document — much as a conjuror might help one of his audience to materialize a rabbit from a hat.

The assignment had cost him several sleepless nights. Even now, outwardly calm, he was a mass of nerves. So much could go wrong. The Princess might ask a question he couldn't answer. He might dry up like an actor on the first night. The chronic cold which he suffered each winter might drown his exposition in a welter of incomprehensible coughs and sneezes.

The telephone rang. He jumped as though bitten by a cobra. He had forbidden all phone calls until the royal party was safely off the premises.

In the outer office his secretary, hand over the mouthpiece, explained:

'Paternoster Room.'

'For crying out loud! Tell 'em to — '

He checked himself. The girl was unlikely to pass on the message he had conceived. Instead he said irritably:

'They know I'm not taking calls!'

'It's Mr Wigmore.'

The assistant keeper's outward composure began to disintegrate.

'What the hell does *he* want?'

Kevin Wigmore was the key figure in the Paternoster Room where the documents ordered by readers through the computer were loaded into something resembling a miniature railway system for delivery to the Reading Room. His job was really that of station-master who had to ensure the smooth running of the lines. He had assistants who located and dispatched the documents, but if the station-master was not at his post, if something had gone wrong in the Paternoster Room . . .

'It's not him on the phone,' replied his secretary patiently. 'It's Mr Harvey — *about* Mr Wigmore.'

'*What* about him?'

'Hasn't been in today.'

'Christ! Not *again*! Why the hell wasn't I told?'

'You said no calls, Mr Pepperbred.'

The assistant keeper groaned. As he seized the telephone to find an instant replacement for the missing Wigmore an agitated superior officer put his head round the door.

'Come on, man! She's here!'

Pepperbred cast a despairing look at his secretary as if begging her to do something — anything — to avert the impending disaster. If the system failed to produce a document for the Princess — if no rabbit came out of the hat — he would be the laughing-stock of the office.

*   *   *

Miraculously, from the moment the royal party were received everything went without a hitch. The Princess was shown how readers fed their reader cards into the turnstile to gain admission to the Reading Room and record their presence with the computer. They went up to the Reading Room where a sea of octagonal tables gave the illusion of a vast honeycomb. The bees, readers deep in the documents spread before them, were a cross-section of humanity. All races and all colours. Bespectacled Americans. Moustachioed central Europeans. Bearded Africans. Shapely saried Indians. Shapeless muu-muued Caribbeans.

All ages and professions. Schoolboys on A-level projects. Post-graduates laying the foundation of an academic career. Professors working on the monograph that would set the seal on their reputation and confound those who dared to question their pet theory. Historical novelists seeking local colour from past centuries. Retired soldiers, sailors and airmen reliving their professional careers and writing their memoirs. 'Record agents' — merchant scholars providing a research service for people who could not come to London. All busily extracting nectar — or poison — from the nation's archives.

Michael Carrington, surrounded by sixteenth-century State papers and statutes dealing with the vice of gambling and the virtue of archery, was established at a table in the area set aside for those readers who wanted to use typewriters. The idea was that the competing voices of many typewriters would somehow cancel each other out and cease to be heard by any individual typist. If there ever was anything in this theory it had been disproved by the arrival of Carrington a month or two earlier. Although he used only two fingers his speed was incredible. His machine rattled like a Sten gun and was painfully audible the length and breadth of the typing area. Looks of disapproval from his immediate neighbours failed to stem the fusillade and within two days of his arrival they had all withdrawn to the furthest vacant tables.

Bodley's reappearance in the Reading Room had surprised Carrington, but the latter's attempt to establish friendly relations met with a pointed rebuff. Bodley knew he was behaving badly, for he was no worse off as a result of Carrington's treatment — indeed he was a hundred pounds better off for the two weeks he had worked for his friend; but somehow he could not avoid associating Carrington with his troubles. On the occasions when they met they did no more than exchange a distant nod.

Today Bodley was deep in a Colonial Office Malta volume — a foolscap tome bound in decaying brown leather with line after line of neat faded copperplate covering six hundred dog-eared leaves. It was a report of His Majesty's Commissioners for enquiring into the affairs of the island in the year 1812. He hadn't even known who this particular royal was and it was only after an ashamed peep in a reference book that he identified him as George III.

He was painstakingly transcribing what seemed to him to be the most significant passages, and much to his surprise finding them amusing. The Commissioners had recorded that 'it was a matter of gratulation to find that the great mass of the people were happy and contented; warm in their professions of attachment to Great Britain; and thriving in wealth and population to a degree almost unprecedented'. Even so it had not been all sweetness and light. 'The Higher Orders whose stationary revenues have not kept pace with the general increase in wealth look with a somewhat jealous eye on the prosperity which surrounds them; and it is from this class that a small leaven of discontent has arisen.'

'Splendid!' murmured Bodley. 'Differentials were a problem even in those days.'

'Sh!' There came a viperous hiss from the lady at the neighbouring seat.

Peter Plumb found himself sitting at the same table as Alistair Macalister, at whose tutorial feet he had sat three years earlier. He found their meeting slightly embarrassing for he had not missed William Hickey's piece in the *Daily Express* a month or two ago which did full justice to the fracas at MIL's party to launch their history. He also knew that many questioned whether true scholarship could be reconciled with Macalister's burning ambition to add to his bank balance rather than to human knowledge, and that when his lucrative commission from MIL had been announced many heads were shaken in the Senior Common Rooms of Oxford and Cambridge. No scholar and gentleman would undertake such an enterprise. The young man was relieved when Macalister departed, saying he had an appointment in the City at noon. His departure was so sudden that Peter suspected that his late tutor was equally embarrassed by their chance meeting and had invented a pretext for escaping.

The Princess was the soul of charm. She listened with attention to Pepperbred's exposition and answers to her questions. His nervousness vanished when he discovered that she was after all a human being. The Lord Chancellor, hovering within earshot, was favourably impressed by his performance.

The royal party glanced with interest at the Press, too intent on their labours to pay heed to the visitor, for once unprofitable copy. The only minor contretemps was not of the authorities' making. When the procession paused to watch some readers at work a greybeard professor with known leftist tendencies was heard to mutter:

'Might as well be in the monkey house at the zoo. Why don't she throw us a royal banana?'

Under Pepperbred's guidance the Princess seated herself at the computer keyboard and with one finger painstakingly tapped out the reference number of one of the documents suggested as being of special interest. She chose the famous map of Calais drawn while the port was still an English possession — worrying since the six-foot document required one of the outsize Paternoster containers which sometimes ran off the rails.

There was no cause for alarm. Pepperbred's trained ear picked up the rumble of invisible machinery which meant that the priceless map was safely on the way.

With a final rumble and bump the container nosed through the trapdoor, like a crematorium in reverse. The counter attendant, a powerful woman in her fifties, clad in the blue uniform of the PRO, stepped forward to unload its cargo.

That her failure to do so was received without a murmur from the assembled company was not due to the many 'Silence!' notices but simply to the fact that all were totally deprived of breath.

The Princess had conjured up, not one of the nation's great treasures, but the defunct body of the master of the paternoster, Kevin Wigmore, his cranium shattered in three distinct places.

4

The reactions to the event just described would provide a student of psychology with raw material for a doctoral thesis.

When the counter attendant, who had just failed to lay out the mortal remains of the late Mr Wigmore before Her Royal Highness, recovered her breath she emitted a succession of piercing shrieks and was led away to the First Aid Room for suitable treatment.

The Princess, trained to take in her stride the most improbable turn of events, was for once out of her depth. Regrettably her mentors had not foreseen an occurrence of this nature in her official life. She was therefore at a loss to know what protocol demanded of her.

The Lord Chancellor, accustomed to make quick decisions, came to her rescue. Followed by her lady in waiting, private secretary, and detective he propelled her with indecent haste towards the stairs. He was moved as much by his own anxiety to escape as by any wish to save the royal visitor from further embarrassment. He led the quartet to their waiting cars and told the drivers to return home without delay.

Then, reminding himself that as minister in charge of the public records he must appear to take some interest in a murder committed among them, however distasteful it might be, instead of quietly slipping back to Westminster as he had intended, he steeled himself to return to the scene of the crime.

The keeper, deputy keepers and other officials in the entourage, with their more immediate responsibility for the orderly conduct of affairs in the office, were naturally aghast. They had no difficulty in identifying their late colleague, in spite of his fearful injuries — but how on earth had he got himself into this unbelievable position? Who could possibly have wanted to kill him? Above all, why take the bizarre step of loading him into the paternoster?

Pepperbred made his way to the

nearest telephone and told the switchboard to call the police. As he did so he was ashamed to find himself wondering who he would recommend for promotion to fill the unexpected vacancy in the paternoster department, and, even more shameful, how would this untoward happening affect his own promotion prospects.

The few readers who had not left their places to watch the royal progress now flocked to see what was up. One of the older researchers regaled his companions with the hoary legend of a former Keeper of the Public Records who had disappeared in the stack rooms never to be seen again. Maybe the paternoster had dredged up his mummified body? He was reminded, however, that the legend related to the cavernous vaults of the old Record Office in Chancery Lane. The few keepers who had commanded at Kew were all well and truly accounted for.

The three security men brought in to guard the Princess thanked their stars she was not the victim.

Predictably the most violent reaction

came from the ladies and gentlemen of the Press. The screams brought them from their thirty-year-old files back to the present day like a pack of hounds scenting the kill. Their collective eye took in at a glance what had happened and in an instant a dozen interviews were taking place, and a dozen startling headlines were conceived for next morning's papers.

Pepperbred, sensing that things were getting out of hand, ordered the counter staff to close the aluminium shutters separating the paternoster terminus from the Reading Room; and then swiftly took himself to the public address system in the entrance hall.

'Ladies and gentlemen,' he said, surprised at the steadiness of his voice, 'as some of you will know there has been an accident in the Reading Room. The police will be here shortly. Until then please remain in your places.'

Hardly had he switched off the microphone when a large American bustled up — Hiram Thrasher, an associate professor at Longmead College,

Maryland, with whom he had several dealings in the last few weeks. He was writing a monograph on the origins of the American War of Independence and had needed help in threading his way through the contemporary British papers.

'See here, Mr Pepperbred,' he said breathlessly. 'I'm darned if I know what goes on — I just came in to collect these photocopies.' He patted a fat envelope under his arm. 'I've got exactly sixty minutes to get to Heathrow, so I'm leaving now. OK?'

The assistant keeper was surprised. He had believed that the American was due to stay in England until the end of January. He thought rapidly. The police might want to interview readers but he had no authority to detain them.

'I can't ask you to stay, Mr Thrasher. We have your address — should we need to get in touch.'

'You said something about an accident on the public address?' said the other curiously as he collected hat and a huge fur coat from the cloakroom.

'A colleague has been killed.'

'Killed?'

'In fact, it looks like murder.'

'What d'ye know! Anyhow, thanks for all your help. Back again in the summer.'

The American wrung Pepperbred's hand painfully and left the building like a grizzly on the run. As he disappeared the assistant keeper wondered if he had been right to let him go. He consoled himself with the thought that there was really no way of stopping him.

Before he could return to the Reading Room a police car drew up at the entrance. The larger of the two occupants introduced himself:

'Inspector Robinson. This is Sergeant Tough. Now, what's this all about? The girl who called us didn't seem to know.'

As he led the policemen up the staff staircase Pepperbred explained. The inspector whistled and said:

'My, my! In the middle of a royal visit!'

'I've asked everybody to stay.'

'Good. Somebody left as we arrived,' observed the inspector. 'In a devil of a hurry.'

'An American professor. We get a lot of

them at this time of year. Had a plane to catch. I couldn't stop him,' Pepperbred added defensively.

The inspector grunted.

The body still lay in the coffinlike paternoster wagon. Robinson had a brief look and said:

'Not much doubt about that! Get on to Doc Middlehurst, Jim. *And* the photographer. *And* the fingerprint boys. Tell 'em to put their skates on. Now, Mr — '

'Pepperbred.'

' — I'd better see the boss first.'

'The keeper? He's in his office. With the Lord Chancellor. He was here to receive the Princess, you know; and he sent her away when — when this happened.'

The keeper recounted the events of the morning at rather greater length than Pepperbred. The inspector listened patiently and when he had finished asked:

'Any idea why?'

'None. Pepperbred?'

'No, sir. No reason at all.'

'Somebody had a reason,' murmured the inspector. 'Was he on good terms with the rest of the staff?'

'Yes — though his job didn't bring him much into contact with them. He worked behind the scenes.'

'In charge of delivering the documents?'

'And managing the surveillance system.'

The inspector pricked up his ears.

'Surveillance?'

'We keep an eye on readers — through TV cameras above each table.'

'Big Brother, eh?' observed the inspector tactlessly.

The keeper bristled.

'We have a duty to preserve an important part of our national heritage. Arguably the most important part. If only you realized what readers can get up to. Spilling ink, leaking ballpens, leaning on documents, snack lunches, making tracings. If they thought no one was looking they'd get away with murder.'

'Murder?'

'A figure of speech,' went on the keeper hastily. 'I was referring only to their treatment of the documents. In fact, a reader can't have anything to do with

Wigmore's death.'

'Why not?'

'The murder obviously took place in the stackroom — '

'Stackroom?'

'Where the records are housed — and where the paternoster railway starts. Staff working there have a special badge with their photograph. Anybody without a badge — a reader — would be spotted. And there's only one way in.

I wonder, thought the inspector. Badges could be faked. The keeper went on with a slight note of sarcasm:

'However, the readers await your pleasure. About two hundred of them this morning, I reckon. To interview them all — say ten minutes each — ' he paused to do a mental calculation — 'should take no more than thirty hours.'

'Let 'em go — unless anybody wants to make a statement,' said the inspector mildly. 'But take their names and addresses.'

'No need,' replied the keeper. 'The computer knows who is here. You can have the print-out whenever you like.'

The inspector seemed surprised. He looked at his sergeant.

'Sergeant Tough's a computer buff. What d'ye think, Jim?'

'Should be no problem, sir.'

'OK. Send 'em all home.'

'What about tomorrow?' asked Pepperbred. 'Do we open as usual?'

The keeper looked questioningly at the inspector.

'It can be business as usual, so far as we're concerned,' said Robinson. 'It will probably be a help to see your systems as they usually operate. It would be useful to have a *pied-à-terre* for a few days.'

'A murder headquarters?' said the keeper knowledgably. 'That can be arranged.'

As Pepperbred left the room to release the captive readers the inspector said:

'If you rule out a reader, it leaves only the staff.'

The keeper had not yet arrived at the logical conclusion of his blanket exoneration of the readers and looked disconcerted. The Lord Chancellor, who had listened attentively to these exchanges, thought it time to intervene.

'I am of course less familiar with the lay-out of the office and the procedures than is the keeper, but it does seem to me that *anyone* willing to take a risk could get into the stack rooms. Breaches of security occur in establishments where the arrangements are much tighter than they need to be here, and where the consequences for the national interest could be much graver than — '

'Simple murder,' put in the inspector.

'The point I am trying to make,' went on the Lord Chancellor coldly, 'is that in spite of what the keeper has said, which seems very reasonable, we must keep an open mind. And no doubt you'll do just that, Inspector. We can't rule anybody out — reader, member of the staff, possible outsiders. Now, if you'll excuse me?'

'Certainly, sir. May I call on you at your convenience for a formal statement?'

'By all means, Inspector.'

The Lord Chancellor withdrew, followed by the keeper. The inspector, unaccustomed to dealing with ministers of the Crown, heaved a sigh of relief.

Downstairs the ladies and gentlemen of the Press were fighting each other for the three public telephones to get their stories through. Peter Plumb, showing enterprise and cunning beyond his years, used one of the official phones in the Reading Room, deserted in the general excitement, to call the duty editor in the BBC TV News Room and give him a brief summary of the morning's events.

'Any point in sending a camera crew?' he was asked.

'I doubt it. They're closing the building now. ITN are in luck. They filmed the arrival of the royal party. But there must be some PRO footage in the library. There was a news item when the Kew office opened — and *Panorama* and *Nationwide* have featured it since then.'

He hung up with the satisfied feeling that although he had not advanced his own project by a single shipwreck, he had earned his keep.

5

Shortly after noon on that bitterly cold December day, at almost exactly the moment when Kevin Wigmore achieved his unscheduled presentation to royalty, Sir Maurice Dyer's secretary announced that Alistair Macalister was in the outer office, anxious to see him. Although Peter Plumb had been right in surmising that the historian was embarrassed by their chance meeting in the Public Record Office it was not in fact the reason for his sudden departure from Kew. The visit to his employer had been planned for some days.

'He says it's urgent, sir.'

'How the *hell* can it be urgent?' the chairman demanded angrily. 'Told me the other day we shouldn't see him again for a couple of years. Not before he's finished the book.'

Dyer was accustomed to use the dead period between Christmas and the New

Year to attend to personal affairs hitherto neglected, and he did not take kindly to an enforced variation of routine. He went on ungraciously:

'Oh, all *right*. Give him five minutes. No more. And it mustn't become a habit. Next time put him on to Muir.'

The historian entered the chairman's room wreathed in smiles, with a jaunty step, apparently oblivious of the fact that his visit was less than welcome.

'Well?' said Dyer, hardly allowing him time to sit down. In spite of his purposeful entrance Macalister seemed uncertain how to begin. Then he collected himself and, still smiling, said:

'I'll come to the point right away, sir. When we last met I said the art of the historian is distilling the truth from complementary sets of documents.'

'I remember,' responded Dyer testily. 'To make an atomic explosion, you said.'

'*You* said,' corrected Macalister. 'At the time I disagreed. But as it turns out, *I* was wrong. *You* were right. Remarkably right!'

'How d'ye mean?'

'The firm's papers illustrate MIL's great contribution in World War II. The vital part it played in winning the war.'

'Of course. Nothing new in that. When he visited us after the war Winston Churchill said we'd been one of the keys to victory. That's partly why we want our history to be written.'

'On the other hand, the War Office and Ministry of Supply papers show the part the civil servants played.'

'Common ground,' said Dyer irritably, keeping his temper with difficulty. 'What *are* you driving at?'

The telephone rang. Dyer's secretary murmured discreetly:

'Five minutes, sir.'

'Thank you, Miss Grigg. No calls for the time being, please. Now, for heaven's sake, man, come to the point. I'm busy.'

If possible, Macalister's smile became broader. He said:

'When your papers and the official records are read together — which is what I've been doing for the last month — some curious discrepancies emerge.'

'Hardly surprising. There *was* a war on,

you know. You haven't come in specially to tell me *that*?'

'I'm afraid we can't blame the war for these particular discrepancies,' Macalister went on unmoved. 'In brief, Ultra Special Alloys Limited, one of MIL's subsidiary companies, deliberately swindled the government out of many million pounds.'

There was a profound silence while Dyer allowed this to sink in. Then he cried:

'Impossible! Nobody could get away with that!'

'Impossible it may be,' replied Macalister coolly, 'but it happened all right. The figures are crystal clear. Even to me, and I used to get nought for arithmetic.'

'I simply don't believe it,' persisted Dyer. 'Couldn't be done.' He glared angrily at the historian. 'At least not without collusion — on the grand scale.'

'Shrewd,' observed Macalister patronizingly. 'Very shrewd. That's precisely what happened. All beautifully covered up. Both the government accountants and yours were taken for a splendid ride. Mind you, as you said just now, it wasn't too difficult in wartime. With bombs dropping on all sides everybody's arithmetic tended to become careless. Key documents could be destroyed by enemy action. Sometimes very conveniently. Curious coincidence that you were in one of the departments concerned.'

Dyer was outraged.

'You're not suggesting *I* was involved?'

'No, no. It was just coincidence; but it would have been rather bad luck if you *had* been in Contracts Division.'

'Didn't those concerned run a terrible risk? The fraud was bound to come out.'

'At the time they thought they were quite safe. The papers were all top secret, and in those days secret papers were withheld for fifty years. So unless any of them intended to live to a hundred they were home and dry. As it turned out, none of them survived the thirty years after which secret papers may now be read by the public.'

'That's something,' murmured Dyer.

'But the firm is still there,' Macalister continued relentlessly. 'For good measure some major military operations failed because of the phoney contracts to which Ultra Special Alloys was a party. The army had to rely on non-existent supplies from the firm. Which was embarrassing. You will recollect that they specialized in armour-piercing shells.'

'If this is true — '

'It's true,' said the historian patiently. His smile suggested he might be paying the chairman the most gracious of compliments.

'Can it be proved?'

'To your complete satisfaction — if that's the right expression.'

'How much was involved?'

'Difficult to say. At least ten million. Say a hundred million at today's prices.'

'Well, well,' said Dyer, at last accepting that he was confronted with fact. 'If there *are* skeletons in the cupboard it's just as well that a member of the family should unearth them. I'm not sure where the firm stands over irregularities of forty years ago — '

'Irregularities!'

Macalister was amused. His smile was converted into a burst of laughter.

'There's another irregularity I must mention. One of the officials suspected that all was not well. He made a comprehensive analysis of the contracts, and left on the file a pretty damning memorandum.'

'Nothing was done about it?'

'Not at the time. The file was closed in August 1944 and put away with the other secret files.'

'Didn't the official follow the thing up?'

'Two days after the date of his memorandum he was killed by a flying bomb. In Croydon. But he lived in Harrow and there was no reason why he should be in Croydon at the time of the incident.'

'Perhaps a woman?' said Dyer hopefully.

'I've seen his family — son and daughter. They still think the thing a mystery, and they'd very much like to know the truth.'

'So?'

'That flying bomb was very convenient for USAL.'

'You're not suggesting — ?'

'But I am. The author of that memorandum was put out of the way. Thanks to the facilities kindly provided by the then enemy. He was killed and left, suitably damaged, where the flying bomb landed.'

'Good God! But this memorandum — '

'Not to worry! I removed it from the file. I may say at considerable risk to my career. If I'd been caught in the act, I'd have been banned for life from the PRO, and you can see what that would mean to a professional scholar. I took a very big chance — on your behalf.'

He threw a folder on the chairman's desk.

'There you are. A photocopy. Have a look at it at leisure, but if I may presume to advise, don't ask your accountants to analyse it. They're an honest breed and might ask awkward questions. Or for that matter, anybody else. There's safety in silence.'

'My dear fellow!' said Dyer, now feeling he had been hauled from a quicksand in the nick of time. 'My dear, dear fellow! I can't tell you how grateful I am — how grateful my board will be. We shall certainly want to express our gratitude in some tangible form, especially as I doubt whether we shall now go ahead with our history. There will also be the matter of compensation, which may not be adequately covered in your contract.'

'Most generous,' murmured Macalister, flashing yet another smile on his employer.

'Of course, you appreciate I'll have to discuss with my board.'

'Quite. Though we don't want to involve too many people, do we?'

'Fortunately Sir Bernard Mitchell is an accountant. So we can get expert advice from within the board.'

'Most helpful.'

'Shall we meet again — say this day fortnight?'

As he passed through the outer office Macalister favoured Miss Grigg with one of his most resplendent smiles. It must have been a very cordial meeting, she thought, in spite of her boss's first reaction.

★ ★ ★

As the District train pulled out of Kew Gardens Station Peter Plumb was struck by an idea that seemed entirely outrageous. At Turnham Green it was remotely possible, at Hammersmith sensible and enterprising, and when the Shepherd's Bush travolator carried him down to the shopping precinct en route for Kensington House, positively brilliant.

When he put it to Jeremy Whitaker, the producer for whom he worked, it was instantly dismissed in a cloud of tobacco smoke.

'My dear infant! Not on your nelly! Simply because you stumble on a bizarre murder you suggest that vast sums of the corporation's hard-won income should be put at your disposal to make a documentary? A documentary that will have no ending if the murderer is not caught? *Hamlet* without the Prince!'

'We take a chance on that.'

'As you are well aware, our miniscule budget is planned a year ahead. There's no money for a twelfth-hour harebrained programme — even if I supported it.'

'As *you* are well aware, there is the controller's contingency fund to take care of twelfth-hour brainwaves. *And* there's a precedent.'

'Thank God, we're not Whitehall. *What* precedent?'

'*Police*. That programme when we sat down live with Thames Valley Police, no holds barred.'

Whitaker affected to be overcome with astonishment. When he had recovered he said:

'You aspire to follow one of our most respected and innovative producers? You, a RAT — '

'TAP,' interrupted Peter.

It should be explained for the benefit of the uninitiated that Peter Plumb had been engaged by the BBC as a research assistant trainee (RAT), which designation a sensitive Establishment Department had replaced with the less rodential trainee assistant producer.

'A RAT by any other name smells just as foul,' said Whitaker philosophically, puffing his pipe into life again. 'But you are a *persistent* RAT. With some intelligence. And energy. Oh, to be young and energetic! Very well. Put your harebrained idea on one side of an A4 sheet, and I, kindly superior that I am, will lay it before the head of department.'

'With your support?'

'I shan't waste his time by putting up a proposal and then helping him to shoot it down.'

'Bless you, Jeremy.'

'Whether the head of department will put it to the controller is another matter.'

To Whitaker's surprise and Plumb's delight both head of department and controller reacted favourably. Whitaker was instructed to cost the programme, and more tricky, to get the agreement of the Metropolitan Police and the authorities of the Public Record Office. These objectives were attained within twenty-four hours — essential if the programme was to get off the ground. Peter Plumb, RAT turned TAP, found himself in charge of BBC television's first murder investigation, in command of a camerman, assistant camerman, sound recordist, lighting technician and Girl Friday. When he went to bed that night he wondered if he had bitten off more than he could chew.

6

The *pied-à-terre* found for Inspector Robinson and Sergeant Tough was the office of an assistant keeper on leave. The inspector already had a nasty feeling he was going to be out of his depth. A big man, with square shoulders and massive biceps straining at the sleeves of his off-the-peg trilon, he looked as if he might have had a more profitable career in the all-in wrestling ring. He had acquired a reputation for profound thought by the simple expedient of maintaining a wooden expression at all times and revealing his thoughts only at long intervals when he was certain he was right.

He had come up through the ranks after pounding a beat in V Division and was therefore very much a home product. The few murders passing through his in-tray had been run-of-the mill affairs — fatal muggings, jealous husbands, armed bank raids and the like. None had presented a serious intellectual challenge. Nearly all had been solved by team-work and routine police methods.

This affair, a murder in a government department, was a different kettle of fish. The scholarly atmosphere, the inevitable interest of television and the national Press, the computerization of the organization which had been the subject of world-wide publicity when the new building opened a year or two earlier — everything was out of the ordinary. Robinson's foreboding was increased by his sergeant's qualifications. Not only had Tough taken a degree at the Open University (almost insubordination, when his superiors had left school at sixteen and not opened a textbook since) but he actually owned his own mini-computer and was a considerable bore in the station mess with his endless talk of bits and memories and crashed programs — whatever they might mean.

However, the inspector was on familiar ground when questioning a human witness about the death of a fellow human being. He listened carefully whilst Ernest Pepperbred recited from the murdered man's personal file:

'Kevin Wigmore. Age 35. Married with two children. Incidentally, his wife used to work in the old Public Record Office at Chancery Lane. Been with us for fifteen years. First at Chancery Lane, and then moved here when the new office opened, it being more convenient for him transport-wise — '

'Has his wife been told?' interrupted the inspector.

'The keeper phoned her — I hope that was all right?'

'What sort of a chap was he?'

'Pretty average — except I suppose he was more ambitious than most. But he wasn't a ball of fire. Didn't like his present job. Would have liked it better to be in the public eye, but *somebody*'s got to do the behind-the-scenes jobs. In any case, he was due for a move.'

'Was there anything unusual about his behaviour lately?'

'Not really — except I suppose that with hindsight — '

'Yes?'

'In the last two months he began to take the odd day at short notice. Nothing wrong with that as he had plenty of leave in hand. But it was unpopular with the people who had to stand in for him. There was a bit of a row.'

'Serious?'

'Oh, no. Just the usual office grumble.'

'I see. Now, can we have a look at this paternoster thing?'

The door leading from the Reading Room to the stackroom was a massive steel affair worthy of a top-security prison, hidden from a large part of the Reading Room by a concrete buttress which the inspector saw could make it easier for an intruder to get in unobserved, with or without a special badge.

'The only way in?'

'Yes. As a security measure,' said Pepperbred. He went on: 'The door has two locks. The main one is a Chubb used when the office is closed. There's a simple spring lock for use during office hours. All the staff who have to use the stackroom have keys to it.'

The inspector looked puzzled.

'But the door's open now?'

'Yes,' Pepperbred conceded defensively. 'We do keep it open. To save trouble. Most of the assistant keepers have to go in two or three times a day. They may want to consult a record without waiting for the computer to send it. Or they may have to go through a series of twenty or thirty records to find out which one they want. It would be a waste of effort to bring them all out.'

'So there would be a fair amount of traffic — in and out? Which would make it easier for some unauthorized person to get in?'

'It could also make it more difficult,' countered Pepperbred. 'Increase the chance of being spotted.'

The Paternoster Room was like a railway station with two lines disappearing into a tunnel. On one line the 'wagons' were red plastic containers about two feet long lined up ready to receive the smaller records and carry them down to the Reading Room. On the other, the wagons were six feet long, twins of the one used to deliver the unfortunate Wigmore.

'I suppose he was attacked round about here,' said Pepperbred.

'No doubt,' agreed the inspector. He had already noticed an unpleasant stain on the bare concrete floor a few feet behind the assistant keeper. The latter went on:

'It would be easy enough to lift a body into the container. Then all you have to do is press the 'Forward' button on the control panel to send the container into the tunnel. It would remain there out of sight until somebody ordered a large document. So when the Princess ordered the map of Calais it took second place in the queue — *behind* the wagon with the body.'

'I understand,' said Robinson. 'Doesn't this suggest inside knowledge? How to operate the system?'

'The controls are clearly marked, as you can see. And we have weekly tours — groups from the universities, learned societies and so on — when the system is demonstrated.'

'Dozens of people would know how to start the machinery?'

'More like hundreds. We keep a record of these groups. You'd like to see it.'

'Might be useful,' said Tough.

'While you're here,' said Pepperbred, 'you'd better look at the surveillance system. That was Wigmore's other job.'

He led the way to a small adjoining office where the main feature was a TV monitor screen. He switched it on to show an overhead view of Table No. 1, now without readers. He turned a dial to bring the other tables into view in succession.

'Wigmore could keep an eye on *all* readers,' said Tough. 'Although they didn't know of his existence?'

'There's no secret about the surveillance system,' replied Pepperbred. 'The TV cameras above every table are there for all to see. But of course readers didn't know who was actually at the receiving end. Wigmore kept a record of people mishandling documents so we could warn them to be more careful in future. In serious cases we would consider withdrawing a reader's card.'

'May we see his record?'

Pepperbred hunted through the desk drawers.

'Here.'

He handed over a large cardboard bound Stationery Office notebook.

'The odds must be against spotting a reader breaking the rules,' said Tough as he flipped through the pages. 'I mean, if you watch only one table at a time, you can't tell what's happening at the others.'

'True enough,' admitted Pepperbred. 'What's more, the surveillance is carried out only for short spells. It's really the threat of a spot check that matters. I've no doubt dozens of strange things go unnoticed.'

'What happens if somebody *is* spotted?'

'The assistant keeper on duty in the Reading Room is told by phone. He's supposed to tear a strip off the offender and warn him he may lose his reader's card if it happens again.'

'Which could be serious?'

'Yes, indeed. For example, a post-graduate working on a thesis might find it was the end of his career.'

'Did Wigmore actually handle the documents?'

'No. Two assistants do the donkey work. Buchan and Spicer. You'd like to see them.'

Dougal Buchan, a red-haired, red-bearded 25-year-old, was the senior.

'Ooor job,' he said in answer to Robinson's question, 'is tae collect readers' requisition slips as the computer prints them, fin' the documents and load them on tae the paternoster.'

The policemen found his Aberdeen accent difficult.

'Means a lot of walking?'

'We dinna walk,' said the youth pityingly. 'There's seventy miles o' shelves. So we use wee electric cars. We couldna begin tae dee the job wi'oot them.'

'When did you last see Mr Wigmore alive?'

'At fower o'clock — when he went tae tea in the canteen. When we went aff duty.'

'He must have gone back to the

stackroom after tea?'

'Aye. Like he usually did. Tae write up his notes for the day.'

'And when he didn't come in this morning?'

'We thocht he maun be on a day's leave.'

'In spite of the royal visit?'

'He taks a lot o' leave.'

'But you didn't report his absence?'

'Mr Pepperbred said nae calls till efter the royal visit. Forbye we didna need Mr Wigmore. It's oor job tae fin' and load the documents.'

He might have been a trade union leader arguing the case in a demarcation dispute.

Robinson asked:

'Did Wigmore seem worried — not his usual self — in the last few days?'

The young Scot considered for a moment. Then he said cautiously:

'Weel — '

'Yes?'

'He was spending mair time on the surveillance than he usually did.'

'So?'

'We thocht he had his e'e on somebody. One particular reader.'

'Which one?'

'I dinna ken.'

He seemed reluctant to say any more.

'Even if you don't know for sure,' said the inspector, 'a guess might help.'

'Weel. There was this blonde at Table 24. American. Smashin'.'

'You thought Wigmore was keeping her under surveillance — for reasons unconnected with the safe keeping of the public records?'

This was too much for Buchan. Tough translated:

'He was doing a peeping Tom act?'

'That's it,' replied Buchan, relieved that someone else had put his thought into words.

'I see. Now, what about the murder weapon? Seen any sign of it?'

'No. But I ken what it was — what it must hae been. And I ken where ye'll fin' it.'

'You do?'

'It was ane o' yon paperweights. Lead rods covered wi' leather. It wad gie a dunt jist like he got.'

The inspector and sergeant exchanged glances. The latter translated again, this time for the benefit of his superior officer:

'The use of such a paperweight would be consistent with the injuries sustained.'

'I see,' said Robinson. 'Could well be. And where do we find the thing?'

'If it was me,' went on Buchan, now thoroughly enjoying himself, 'I mean, if I had used it, I'd hide it in ane o' yon cardboard boxes.'

He pointed to the shelves outside the Paternoster Room stretching in all directions as far as the eye could see, laden with the boxes in which the records were stored.

'Twa million o' them,' he said proudly, as if he were personally responsible for collecting them. 'It'll tak' ye a day or two tae open them a'.'

This gentle understatement ended Buchan's evidence. His colleague Albert Spicer generally confirmed what he had said, in more comprehensible language, including the suspicion that Wigmore had been paying special attention to somebody, presumed to be the American girl.

The third member of the staff with whom Wigmore had close dealings was Ronald Rollem, the assistant keeper on duty in the Reading Room. Rollem explained that on an ordinary day he would get three or four phone calls from the surveillance officer telling him the seats where documents were being mishandled.

'Oddly enough he reported hardly any in the last fortnight.'

'That surprised you?'

'Not at the time, although I was quite glad. Readers don't like being told what not to do, and it makes me feel like a schoolmaster. I was behind with my correspondence and the less time I spend traipsing round the room ticking off people the better.'

Back in their office Robinson and Tough conferred. The former said:

'General agreement that victim acted strange. Perhaps keeping a special eye on somebody in the Reading Room.'

'The blonde?'

'Maybe. Maybe not. People like to think the worst. For some reason he let up on reporting misbehaving readers. His record book may throw some light on that.'

They were joined by Dr Middlehurst.

'Well?' demanded the inspector. 'How was he done? When? What with? And why?'

'Hoping for a miracle?' asked Middlehurst. 'As usual. First is easy. Three hefty blows — you saw that for yourselves. Any one of them would have done the trick, but the chap wasn't taking any chances. Weapon found yet?'

'No,' said the inspector. 'That young red-head in the Paternoster Room — '

'Buchan,' put in Sergeant Tough.

' — thinks it could have been a paperweight.'

'I know. Showed me a few samples. All shapes and sizes. All lethal. I'm sure he's right — the long thin model fits best. Absolutely ideal!'

'He also thinks it's been hidden in one of the cardboard record boxes. There's two million of them, which makes a haystack if ever there was one. It'll take a devil of a time to go through them all.'

'Can't be done,' said Sergeant Tough. 'At least, not before you retire, sir. Say one minute per box. Two million minutes is 35,000 hours. Four thousand eight-hour days. One man would take ten years — if he didn't go mad first.'

'Or ten men one year,' said Robinson thoughtfully. 'Christ!'

'In any case,' went on Tough. 'It isn't just the boxes. Half the records are bound volumes. The weapon could be shoved behind them. Which means searching seventy miles of shelving.'

'Take my advice — forget the weapon,' suggested Middlehurst. 'In any case, you won't find fingerprints on it.'

'You can't be sure. We *must* look for it.'

'Even if it takes ten years?'

'With luck we could turn it up right away. Anyhow, at least we've got to make a token search.'

'Not only must you investigate,' said Middlehurst, 'you must be seen to be investigating. OK. It's your problem. I wish you joy. Now, as to when — '

'Well?'

'Very interesting. Thanks to the constant temperature and air-conditioning. Rigor had passed off when I saw him, so he was done at least twelve hours earlier. Body heat implies less than twenty-four hours — '

'Yes, yes,' said Robinson impatiently. 'The approximate *time*.'

'I'll have to look at Glaister before I swear to anything,' replied Middlehurst. 'But at this point, I'd say round about five o'clock.'

'On Wednesday afternoon? Just before the office closed?'

'Or just after,' put in Sergeant Tough.

'You'll have my report first thing in the morning,' said Middlehurst.

'Incidentally,' said Robinson as the doctor rose to go, 'what d'ye make of Buchan *and* his bright ideas?'

'How come he has all the answers, you mean? Number one suspect, eh? What was his motive?'

'Maybe promotion.'

Middlehurst laughed heartily.

'If that was a good motive there'd be

precious few civil servants left.'

'Or policemen,' added Tough.

★   ★   ★

The sergeant was assigned the unpleasant task of interviewing Mrs Wigmore. He found No. 17 Quarry Terrace, Raynes Park, a three-bedroom semi-detached badly in need of exterior decoration, which compared unfavourably with his own three-bedroom semi-detached in Lennox Avenue, Kew. The white paint was peeling from the window frames and front door. As he opened the rickety gate and made his way up the short path he was conscious that several pairs of eyes behind lace curtains in the house opposite were scrutinizing him. The news of Mrs Wigmore's sudden bereavement had spread.

Tough, a kindly man, hated interviews like this. It was impossible to balance sympathy with the needs of the investigation. After a brief murmured expression of sympathy he came quickly to the point. When had she last seen her husband?

Lorna Wigmore, whose two children were being taken care of by her next door neighbour, was so self-possessed that Tough wondered if she had somehow been prepared for the tragedy. She said without emotion, almost as if she had been rehearsing her answer:

'Yesterday morning, when he left for work.'

'When he didn't come home last night — you must have been worried. Or did you expect him to be away?'

'I didn't know what to expect. You see, he's been away three or four times in the last few weeks.'

'Overnight?'

'No — just for the day. You see, I rang him up one day to ask about something and they told me he was on leave; but he'd never said anything about it to me. I got a friend in Establishments to look at his leave sheet, and they said he'd had three other days off I didn't know anything about.'

'Didn't you check with the office last night — when he never came home?'

'By that time everybody would have left — except the security guards, and they wouldn't have known anything.'

She paused to collect her thoughts, still very much in command of herself, thought Tough.

'I'm sure he had something on his mind. At first I thought it was our plan to move. You see, we'd decided to buy a house, a bigger house, in Wimbledon. It was really his idea. I was quite happy here, but he was terribly keen on appearances, you know. Thought it would help him in the job if we had a better house. There was no problem about money because my mother left us two thousand pounds, and what with that and the sale of this house . . . Then something terrible happened.'

'Yes?'

'Two months ago we found dry rot in the cupboard under the stairs. It had spread to the upper floor and the whole place is unsafe. Kevin said it would knock thousands off our selling price — if we could find anybody to buy. He was very upset.'

'What was he doing — on those days off?'

'I thought he must have a girl-friend — a sort of consolation for the trouble over the house and the fact that we wouldn't be able to move. Then last week he suddenly seemed to become more cheerful. This made me sure he had a girl-friend — and I asked him outright.'

'What did he say:'

'Just laughed. Seemed to think it was terribly funny. Said I must be crazy and that our troubles would soon be over. I asked him what he meant but he wouldn't say. After that most of the time he seemed like he usually was, but sometimes he was worried and nervous, as if he still had something on his mind. I just didn't understand it.'

'That was only last week?'

'Yes. Then this morning I went to the building society to see if there was something Kevin hadn't told me about; and they said — '

She began to sob, the first sign of any emotion.

'They told me Kevin had drawn out all

102

the money! My mother's money! Without telling me. Every penny of it had gone!'

'You thought your fears about a girl-friend were justified?'

'What else could it be?'

'And now?'

'I don't know what to think. But what did he want money for if it wasn't a woman?'

Sergeant Tough could think of half a dozen things. He said:

'I think we'll have to talk to the building society people. Did you have a joint account?'

'No. I'm not much good at money — that sort of money. I left everything like that to Kevin.'

'Can you give me a note saying it's OK for us to get details of the withdrawals? It may be important.'

Mrs Wigmore slowly wrote out a form of words to the sergeant's dictation; and he departed having murmured some further words of consolation, well aware that no words from him could soften the blow which had just befallen the young woman.

7

When Sergeant Tough, who devoted much of his spare time to science fiction, when he was not playing with his home computer, returned to Fort Ruskin he saw the strange building as a spacecraft awkwardly force-landed on Planet Earth, now vainly trying to generate enough power to escape from terrestrial gravity. The illusion was heightened by the monotonous hum from the adjacent boiler plant and the outward sloping windows of the first-floor Reading Room, through which the navigators of 2001 might be keeping a weather eye open for uncharted planets rather than the trains of the District Railway, barges on the encircling Thames, and the dreary next-door offices of the Inland Revenue sorting department.

He had already seen enough of the electronic wizardry of the new Public

Record Office, in particular the computer, the heart of the institution, to realize that the police were likely to be faced with an entirely novel murder investigation; and he wondered how Inspector Robinson, who had steadfastly resisted all efforts to move him into the computer age, would fare.

'Good!' observed Robinson, when he had heard his report. 'It's taking shape, Jim.'

'I think it is, sir. If you look at the timetable. The Wigmores plan to move house, because of his ambitions. All goes well, until they discover dry rot, which makes their house unsaleable except at a giveaway price. He begins to take the odd day off, and she thinks he's on to another woman. His colleagues are a bit mystified by his occasional absences. He begins to draw on their savings — without telling her.'

'So?'

'So he decides to get rich quick — in the simplest way possible. Puts their savings on the gee-gees.'

'You're guessing?'

'An intelligent guess,' replied the sergeant modestly. 'There were race meetings on all the days he took leave.'

'There are race meetings somewhere or other every day of the year,' objected the inspector. 'In any case, why go to a meeting? There's plenty of convenient neighbourhood betting-shops.'

'You can be recognized in a betting-shop, maybe by a friend who'll tell the wife. Much easier to be anonymous in a crowd. Point is, on the days in question the race meetings were at Kempton Park and Sandown — within easy reach of Raynes Park. He invests the family fortune, and — '

'Blows the lot?'

'It's not difficult,' said the sergeant, feelingly. 'He's now in real trouble. Remember, it is his wife's money he's blown. But he now has a chance to recoup his losses by going into the blackmail business.'

'Using information picked up in his job?'

'Looks like it. He might have come across something nasty through the surveillance. The answer may be in the record he kept. Something worse than doodling on Magna Carta.'

The inspector produced the surveillance notebook from a drawer. He paused before opening it, and said:

'By the way, how come you know so much about horse-racing?'

The sergeant had the grace to blush.

'I do have an occasional flutter, sir. Nothing against it in Regulations — and it comes in handy sometimes. Background knowledge, I mean.'

They examined the surveillance record together. It was in effect a large diary, with a page for each day. On most days there were three or four entries, giving simply the Table number and a brief note of the offence: '38 C — leaning on document'; '20 E — using fountain pen'; '40 A — eating chocolate'; and so on.

'Twenty offences a week on average,' observed the inspector, 'but only three in the two weeks before the murder. What d'ye make of that?'

'There are fewer readers during the holiday season?' replied Tough.

'That shouldn't change the total all that much.'

'Maybe it was the Christmas spirit. Live and let live.'

'Buchan told us Wigmore was busier than ever at the monitor — he thought watching his blonde.'

'He might have been shielding somebody.'

'He might overlook an offence by a friend — but why shield twenty people? No he had something on his mind all right. We'd better check out the three offenders he did record. You can get their names from the computer?'

'Yes.'

'And check out the American beauty, even if she isn't on Wigmore's list.'

'Assess her charm factor?'

'Something of the sort. If she's all that smashing, Buchan — and Mrs Wigmore — may have a point.'

'One man's crumpet is another man's stale bread,' observed Tough, unaccustomed to uttering aphorisms.

'All the same, have a look at her.'

'If you think I'm qualified, sir.'

The sergeant found that Mary Lou Dale of Kansas State University regularly sat at Table 30 G. This morning was no exception; and he had no difficulty in identifying her. She was entirely out of place among the bluestockings of the Reading Room — a luscious orchid in a field of ageing thistles and withered dandelions. The cover of *Playboy Magazine* would have been a better home. Buchan and Spicer could well have imagined her the innocent star of Wigmore's surveillance show.

Tough so reported to the inspector. He added:

'I can't believe she's got anything to do with this business.'

'I see. She's made another conquest.'

'She's attached to the Institute of Historical Research. Writing a Ph.D. thesis. She's been working here for eighteen months — and she's never been in any trouble over the handling of documents.'

'Doesn't mean a thing,' said the inspector unsympathetically. 'If Wigmore was sweet on her he wouldn't record her misdemeanours. What about the three he *did* report in the last two weeks?'

'Lieutenant Colonel Hector Moberley-Clarke. Michael Carrington. And Miss Christina Fowler. We'd better ask Rollem about them.'

Ronald Rollem was grateful for the leavening of his daily round — answering boring letters from scholars at the opposite ends of the earth, policing the Reading Room, making the occasional foray at the behest of the surveillance officer — occasioned by the murder investigation. He confirmed that he had formally reprimanded the three individuals identified in Wigmore's record, and warned them that there must be no repetition of their offence.

'Had a rough time with Colonel Moberley-Clarke,' he said with a reminiscent grin. 'Using a fountain pen and refused to change to pencil. Said he'd written the reports himself using the same pen when he was in the War Office. He'd used ink then, so why the hell shouldn't he use ink now? No dunghill beetle of a civil servant was going to tell him what to do. I said there had been nothing to stop him doodling all over his precious reports in 1940 but they were now the property of the nation. I thought he'd have a fit, but he calmed down when I said I'd have him thrown out if he didn't put his pen away.'

Rollem smiled happily, savouring the rare victory of a private over a brass hat.

'What about Carrington?'

'Caught using a biro, which can leak and ruin a document. He apologized and said he didn't have a pencil. Told him to buy one at the reception desk downstairs, which he did without a murmur.'

'And the lady:'

'*She* was typing, using Snopake for corrections. Spill a bottle of that on a file and it's real disaster. She was angry, but agreed not to bring the stuff in again.'

Rollem was returning to his duties when the inspector called him back.

'Apart from these cases, did you spot anything unusual on Wednesday?'

'No. I go round the room two or three times in the morning and again in the afternoon, but that puts the old hands on their best behaviour.'

'How d'ye mean?'

'Well, if somebody's sucking a sweet, they'll stop until I've got my back to them. Just like a schoolboy might do.'

'When we arrived here yesterday,' said Robinson, 'we saw somebody — an American professor, I think Mr Pepper-bred said — dashing off in a great hurry. Going to catch a plane. Know anything about him?'

'Very distinguished scholar. Left wing. Been coming here for years. He consulted me about an index on Wednesday afternoon. Surprising, as he knows his way round here better than most. You don't think he — ?'

'Thanks very much, Mr Rollem.'

The assistant keeper accepted his dismissal with good grace.

'I think we can forget about these people,' said the inspector. 'The military gentleman might have been tempted to murder Rollem, hardly Wigmore. Don't suppose he knew of his existence — until he appeared on Thursday morning.'

* ★ ★

The murder in the Public Record Office inevitably sent the popular Press soaring into their seventh heaven. Any down-to-earth murder was a welcome change from the diet of rape, industrial unrest and militant peace protest they had recently been compelled to feed to their readers; but one in which the victim was laid at the feet of royalty in response to a royal computerized command was too good to be true. They made the most of it.

Every correspondent who had ever fed a reader card into the Reading Room turnstile at the PRO wrote an article 'by a leading expert' describing at great length and with little accuracy the world's most up-to-date archive, and usually contrasting it favourably with the National Archives of the United States, still lingering in the steam age. The press gang who had been examining the newly-opened thirty-year-old files were lucky enough to be able to contribute eye-witness accounts. There were interviews with everybody from the senior officials, who said little, down to the junior messenger, who said a lot. The lady who received the body recovered enough to describe her feelings in dramatic detail and was rewarded with a quarter-page photograph in the tabloids.

Even *The Times* acknowledged the event. The usual half inch in the Court Circular letting it be known that the Princess had visited the PRO was speedily transformed into a few inches in the Home News page. It was this that caught the eye of Sir Maurice Dyer as he was driven from Cobham to his tower block in the City the day after the murder. He had already heard about it on the six o'clock news the previous evening, without paying too much attention. Now, however, an idea generated by the more detailed reports was becoming too awful to contemplate.

The instant he reached his office he commanded Gilbert Archer and Bernard Mitchell to meet him there immediately.

He had in any case intended to tell them as soon as possible about Macalister's discovery. He was bound to keep the deputy chairman informed. Mitchell was responsible for the engineering side of MIL; and it was on engineering contracts that the Government had been swindled. Both men had joined MIL after the war and therefore could not be involved in the fraud. When they arrived they left the chairman in no doubt as to their feelings about being dragged into the City on New Year's Eve; but they soon saw he was in a highly nervous state and must be treated gently.

'What's up, Maurice?' asked Archer. 'Are you ill?'

Dyer pulled himself together and gave a brief account of his meeting with the historian the day before.

'Christ!' exclaimed Archer when he had finished. 'We *have* done it this time!'

'He left a photocopy of the memorandum,' said Dyer. 'It's dynamite!'

The others skimmed through the document together. Mitchell said:

'I need more time to look at the small print; but on the face of it it's an open-and-shut case. We're hoist with your petard, Maurice.'

Dyer thought for a moment and then said diffidently:

'I suppose it *is* news to both of you?'

'What the hell does that mean?' demanded Archer angrily.

'You were so much against the history being written. Especially you, Gilbert. Did you suspect something like this?'

'Good God, no! It was just instinct. And how right I was!'

'It's bloody awful,' said Mitchell, who was still thumbing through the memorandum. 'But let's not go off at the deep end. On the credit side — the wartime directors are all dead, I think. For which thank goodness. There'll be no personal scandal for the Press to make hay with. No *live* scandal, anyhow. And as the company didn't profit from the swindle, it can't be liable now. Who d'ye think did organize the thing, Gilbert?'

'Certain names suggest themselves. Two of our predecessors very cleverly made fortunes on the stock exchange, or so the rumour went at the time. Remember?'

'Good heavens!' cried Mitchell.

'Who else?'

'I suppose even if the firm had been technically liable at the time,' said Mitchell, 'we could now invoke the Statute of Limitations.'

'Not for the murder of that civil servant — if he *was* murdered,' said Dyer.

'We didn't do it,' said Archer. 'But I can see there's going to be the most frightful uproar if the whole affair comes out.'

'It's the *other* murder that worries me,' said Dyer.

'What other murder?'

'At Kew. You must have seen the news.'

'During the Princess's visit? said Archer. 'Extraordinary affair. What's it got to do with us?'

'Nothing I hope; but I've been putting two and two together. Macalister, our historian, and self-appointed defender of our reputation, steals a public document on our behalf. I imagine that that rates as a serious crime in any circumstances, but if it's intended to cover up a major wartime fraud . . . '

'We didn't hire him to steal documents,' said Archer. 'That's his lookout.'

'Stealing public documents is one thing,' said Dyer slowly, as if it was too awful to pursue his line of thought. 'Murdering public servants is another.'

'The Kew murder?' said Archer sharply. 'The two things are connected?'

'I don't know the incidence of major crime in the Public Record Office,' said Dyer, 'but two in a matter of days seems above average.'

'You think Macalister killed that young man?'

'I wouldn't bet against it,' said Dyer.

'If you're right,' said Archer, 'it certainly changes the picture. For the sake of argument, he might have been acting as our agent in removing this memorandum, and if that *did* lead him to murder the PRO man, we become accessories after the fact. Where d'ye reckon he stands in all this, Maurice?'

'A little bit like a dog that has just laid a juicy bone at its master's feet. Pleased to have done something clever for his employer. I hinted that we might now have to scrub the history — of course with compensation to him.

'He'll see reason?'

'His reaction was encouraging. In any case, why run the risk of stealing the memorandum if he's *not* on our side?'

'Why indeed?' murmured Archer.

There was something in his tone that made Dyer look at him sharply. The chairman said:

'I've arranged to see him again in a fortnight. To give us time to settle our line.'

'If we're not all behind bars by then,' observed Bernard Mitchell.

On this happy note the three directors dispersed to their several New Year's Eve celebrations.

8

The inquest on Kevin Wigmore, held in the Coroner's Court at Kew, was purely formal. It produced nothing of value for the serried ranks of reporters who crowded into the tiny room. A tearful widow, supported by her sister, gave evidence of identification. A reluctant Pepperbred provided a brief account of the delivery of the body. Dr Middlehurst testified that the injuries made it beyond doubt a case of murder. Inspector Robinson informed the coroner that police enquiries were far from complete, and asked for an adjournment of one month. The coroner agreed and that was that.

In the street outside the court several reporters armed with cheque-books pursued Mrs Wigmore to her sister's waiting car in the hope that they might buy her story. To her eternal credit she would have nothing to do with any of them, no doubt reflecting on the irony of a situation in which her husband's murder could bring her enough cash to buy a mansion exceeding his wildest dreams.

The inquest out of the way, Robinson and Tough got down to their task again. The post-mortem showed that the last food taken by the victim was a somewhat indigestible doughnut, the state of which led the medical experts to put the time of death almost immediately he had returned to the stackroom. He must therefore have been killed between four fifteen, when he was last seen alive, and five o'clock when all readers had left. Only those readers who had lingered until close of play on the Wednesday could be under suspicion.

As there was only one entrance to the stackroom the murderer must have slipped in at some point during the day, not too difficult if he chose his moment carefully; and he must have emerged again before the office closed, rather more risky since he might well walk straight into the arms of half a dozen members of the staff going about their ordinary business. He was certainly no longer in the stackroom. Buchan and Spicer had carried out a lengthy reconnaissance in their 'wee electric cars' to establish that.

The list of readers who had remained late on Wednesday was happily short. Pepperbred explained:

'Usually many more stay until the bell rings. In fact, it's sometimes difficult to get them all out. But what with the holiday season and the weather, that day only the real diehards remained.'

They included several who could not possibly be involved. Four elderly lady record agents whose livelihood depended on the hours they put in at Kew ferreting out information for their clients all over the world, who had not the strength to wield a lethal paperweight, even if they had a motive. A group of schoolboys under the care of their teacher, anxious to make the most of their one day in the PRO. Julian Hardcastle, an established economic historian with half a dozen books to his name in *Who's Who*. The young Oxford don recently appointed to write the history of Megalith Industries

Limited. The two last both working to deadlines and therefore anxious to make full use of the PRO's opening hours. The only other person who seemed remotely qualified to dispose of Wigmore — though why on earth should he want to? — was Richard Bodley, who had begun to work at Kew only a month or two earlier.

'About the time Wigmore began to go off the rails?' said Robinson thoughtfully. 'I wonder?'

It was still theoretically possible that a member of the staff had accompanied Wigmore back to the stackroom, but a complicated series of checks and cross-checks pinpointed the whereabouts of all staff present at the material time and provided them with cast-iron alibis.

Miss Ernestine Dudley, who willingly responded to the police invitation to report anything unusual, explained that she had been in the Reading Room until five minutes to five sitting at the same table as Richard Bodley — the only other occupant of the table.

'Bodley?' said Tough. 'What about him?'

'It may have nothing to do with the

murder,' said the lady, 'but I thought you should know. After all, you did ask about *anything* out of the ordinary. You see, there's a sort of cameraderie among us — the record agents, I mean. Although we make our living searching the records and are therefore competing with each other, we do like to help beginners. Showing them how to use the computer, where to find the indexes they need, and so on.'

'Very commendable,' said the sergeant, suspecting that the lady simply wanted to hold the stage for a few moments.

'Mr Bodley started working here in October, I think. It seemed he was doing a record agent job, working for a Mr Carrington. One or two of us offered to show him the ropes, and we suggested he should register himself as a record agent. To get a share of the business, you know. He said there was no need, as he was working full-time for his friend.'

'Well?'

'Then they had a row. Mr Bodley was told his services were no longer required. It came as a great shock to him, as he really needed the money. You see, his house had been burgled and every single thing removed. *And* no insurance. He couldn't understand why his friend had thrown him overboard.'

'Interesting,' observed Tough, 'but I don't see what it can have to do with the murder,' he added unsympathetically. 'Bodley might want to do away with Carrington, but why Wigmore?'

Miss Dudley was horrified.

'Nothing like that!' she cried. 'It is just that it was so strange. Such bad luck for Mr Bodley. First to lose his furniture — when it was uninsured. Then to get a good job and lose it — for no reason at all, mind you — within a few days. You *did* ask us to let you know if we noticed anything strange.'

'Of course, Miss Dudley. And we're most grateful. I'll certainly pass this on to Inspector Robinson. Meantime, thank you very much indeed.'

Miss Dudley retired, mollified, to continue her researches on behalf of a distinguished American military historian. Tough duly reported what she had said to the inspector, who was not impressed — even when his subordinate reminded him that he himself had remarked on the fact that Bodley's arrival in the PRO had coincided with the beginning of Wigmore's spasmodic absences.

'Probably a dozen people made their first appearance at the same time.'

That, Tough had to admit, was undoubtedly the case.

Two constables had been detailed to search the boxes in the stackroom for the murder weapon — a soul-destroying job which could take literally years. The inspector had perhaps unwisely gone out of his way to explain to the two unfortunates that they were really engaged in a cosmetic exercise — somebody would criticize the police if no attempt was made to find the weapon — and that he reckoned it was a million to one against their finding it. His warning hardly increased their enthusiasm for the task. After three days one of them had the bright idea of using a metal-detector, whereupon Tough had to point out that the presumed weapon was lead, which would not be recognized by a detector.

Happily chance came to their rescue. Professor Hamish Macbride from the University of Aberdeen, who was studying the Union of the Crowns in 1707, ordered a boxful of State papers, which seemed to him to be unduly heavy as he carried it to his table. He had a nasty shock when he undid the tape and found on top of the State papers a paperweight covered with congealed blood and an unpleasant amount of hair.

There were of course no fingerprints, and the discovery told the police no more than Dougal Buchan had already guessed for them. Indeed the only profitable consequence was that the two constables were allowed to stand down while their sanity was still intact. Apart, that is, from the benefit to Peter Plumb's documentary. He prevailed on the Scot to reenact his discovery using an identical box and paperweight, since the originals had been impounded by the police. At first the professor refused point blank to co-operate in such an unscholarly enterprise, but the hint of a fee (small since Peter's budget was none too generous) changed his mind and he provided a useful thirty seconds' worth of film.

For three days Tough ploughed through print-outs and computer document request slips hoping to detect something suggestive — to no avail. The only slight oddity, if Ernestine Dudley's hint of something strange between Bodley and Carrington was discounted, was hinted at, not by the computer, but by the gossip columns of three months ago: the simultaneous presence of the two scholars who had come to blows at the party to launch MIL's history.

'Coincidence, I expect,' said the inspector, gloomily, when Tough reminded him of the incident. 'They might have had a go at *each other* — '

'Like Bodley and Carrington?'

' — but why have a go at Wigmore? There's more to it. But what?'

Tough could not answer the question.

The newspapers were becoming increasingly vocal about the lack of progress in a murder investigation which had promised so much. So also, for different reasons, were Robinson's superiors. Tough, having run the gamut of all the permutations of the print-outs and other material regurgitated by the computer, went back in desperation to the surveillance record — a notebook which any schoolboy could understand without a higher degree in computerization.

He went through it again page by page for the last three months without finding anything suggestive. He was on the point of abandoning the exercise when he glanced idly at the almost blank pages of Christmas week, when the numbers of readers present would be well below average. His desk lamp shone low across the surface of the paper — and then he spotted it.

Monday 20 December which so far he had ignored as a blank page was after all not blank. The slanting rays threw into relief an erasure hitherto invisible. By increasing the angle of the lamp still further it was possible — just — to decipher the erased writing:

'8 H — papers removed.'

Tough could hardly wait for the return of the inspector, who was having coffee in the cafeteria.

'There!' he cried in triumph, thrusting the open notebook under Robinson's nose. 'Take a look at that!'

'A blank page?'

'Hold it at an angle. Somebody wrote '8 H — papers removed' and then rubbed it out. Must have been Wigmore. He saw somebody sitting at 8 H up to something. Recorded it in the usual way and then decided not only not to do anything about it, but actually rubbed out the entry. Why?'

'Maybe he just made a mistake.'

'Then why rub it out so carefully? Because he wanted to keep it to himself.'

Ronald Rollem was unable to help. Wigmore had not reported any improper activity at Table 8 H on the day in question. He did, however, make a suggestion:

'Go through the document request slips from that seat on 20 December. They'll tell you who was sitting there and what files he was using.'

The answer was Julian Hardcastle. In the course of the day he had ordered six files. Five were intact. In the sixth, pages 100 to 120 were missing. The rest of the file contained routine correspondence between the Ministry of Supply and Ultra Special Alloys Limited about World War II contracts.

'It fits, sir,' said Tough in some excitement. 'Wigmore spotted Hardcastle removing these pages. He made a routine note of the offence, and then decided not to report it.'

'Instead he tells Hardcastle he's been caught in the act — '

'Wait a bit,' interrupted Tough. 'Why remove these pages? You can get anything you like photocopied at 10p a page. Why pinch anything?'

'Either you want a souvenir, or more likely you want to suppress the papers,' replied the inspector. 'Either way Wigmore knows he's on to a good thing. Blackmails Hardcastle. Invites him into the stackroom to do a deal and gets knocked on the head for his pains. Body is shoved in the paternoster to keep it hidden as long as possible. Hardcastle waits till coast is clear, nips back into the Reading Room and leaves the building in good order a few minutes before five. How's that?'

'Pretty convincing,' agreed Tough. 'And Hardcastle *was* one of the few people who stayed to the bitter end on the Wednesday. I think we've done it.'

His self-satisfied smile could not have been wider had he won the jackpot at Kempton Park.

9

When he was ushered into the chairman's room Macalister seemed even more cheerful and confident than on his last appearance. He certainly didn't look like a man with murder on his conscience.

'I don't think you've met my colleagues? Mr Archer, deputy chairman. Sir Bernard Mitchell.'

'We did meet briefly. At the party to launch your history.'

'Of course. How stupid.'

Macalister shook hands all round.

'First of all,' began Dyer, trying to appear genial and relaxed, but fiddling nervously with the miniature Toledo sword he used as letter opener, 'let me say how much we appreciate your thoughtfulness in bringing this — ah — this matter to our attention. We have examined the paper you left and we are bound to agree with your conclusion. Some members of the firm — we cannot identify them from the paper — must have been guilty of improper conduct in World War II. No doubt these facts could be passed over in the firm's history, but we have decided that on balance it would be better not to proceed with the book.'

Macalister smiled and said:

'I quite understand. Pity, though. There's still a first-rate book in the making. But I see your position.'

'We see *yours*. It may be embarrassing when a project like this, which has had a great deal of publicity, is cancelled at short notice.'

'One's reputation as a scholar *may* suffer, it is true,' agreed Macalister. 'Unsympathetic critics might hint that the task was beyond one, for example.'

'Therefore we propose to double your fee, as an *ex gratia* measure. I hope that this will be acceptable?'

'Most generous.'

The reply came without hesitation. Dyer's sigh of relief was clearly audible. He said:

'Then that's settled. Your cheque will

be in the post this afternoon.'

'Most generous in normal circumstances, I mean,' said the historian. He awarded each of the three directors a smile in turn. Dyer said:

'Surely the circumstances *are* normal? We have a contract. We decide to cancel as we are fully entitled to do. We are under no obligation to pay you a penny more than the agreed fee — yet we are willing to double it.'

'All true, but — '

'You want to suggest some other arrangement?'

'That is so.'

For a moment Macalister looked like a New Year's Day swimmer summoning up the courage to plunge into an icy pool. He took a deep breath and said:

'I consider that in all the circumstances a reasonable settlement would be a half per cent of the money you swindled the Government out of.'

It took a moment for this to sink in. Then Dyer went white.

'You must be joking!'

'Of course, at current prices.'

The chairman did a rapid mental calculation.

'That's — that's half a million pounds!'

'Exactly. A modest demand, Sir Maurice. The reward for the recovery of stolen goods is ten per cent — ten million pounds in the present case. You're saving nine and a half million.'

Dyer sat back speechless. For a moment he seemed to contemplate using his letter opener for another purpose. Then he said, with difficulty:

'You really *are* serious?'

'These days footballers are bought and sold for a million. *Footballers.* Surely my services — or non-services — are worth half as much? However, if you prefer to make an honest man of MIL, go to the Government and confess your sins. They'll be delighted, and I'll get credit for uncovering a juicy wartime scandal. The Sunday papers will fight for the story, but they won't pay half a million. Which is why you have first refusal.'

The chairman looked despairingly at his two colleagues. Archer said:

'Look here, Macalister. You seem to

think you've got us over a barrel, but may I suggest you think again? There's no point in threatening blackmail if you haven't got something nasty up your sleeve.'

The historian smiled and waited for the other to continue.

'As we see it, you've nothing up your sleeve. The wartime fraud was carried out by individuals long since dead. The firm didn't benefit by one penny. If somebody was murdered as part of a cover-up, for which we've only got your theory, it has nothing to do with us or the firm. So I suggest you accept our offer of compensation, and call it a day.'

'Of course you're right,' replied Macalister, smiling as broadly as ever. 'But there's one thing you seem to have overlooked. Which I find surprising.'

'What?'

'Even a mere historian can read the *Financial Times*. Which has been suggesting that your future depends more than most people realize on landing the missile contract with the Ministry of Defence. And also that half the Cabinet would prefer a much cheaper deal with the Americans. So I guess that if your wartime performance — which probably cost hundreds of Allied lives — becomes public property you'll never smell that contract.'

The three directors were silent. Macalister continued:

'I also guess that there will be a big knock-on effect. You won't be too popular with your Commonwealth customers — or the holier-than-thou Middle East. I think you'll be wise to accept my offer.'

'Suppose we do agree?' said Archer. 'The payment will appear in our accounts. You can't take half a million from petty cash. Questions will be asked. The whole thing will come out.'

Macalister laughed.

'All taken care of. True, we can't rely on a German bomb to destroy the evidence this time — ' the smile grew to Cheshire cat proportions ' — but there's a simple way out.'

'Yes?'

'A ransom demand goes to MIL. Their chairman has been kidnapped. Like the good employer it is, MIL pays up. The chairman, whom the kidnappers have kept in the lap of luxury, no expense spared, is returned bronzed and fit, none the worse for his ordeal. Something of a public hero. It may even put your shares up.'

'Oh, my God!' cried Dyer.

'It may take a little time to get accustomed to the idea,' went on Macalister soothingly, 'but it's the perfect solution. The half million appears in your accounts, no questions asked. Your skeleton is well and truly buried. Your reputation is intact. You've saved millions on the deal. What more d'ye want?'

'What about the police?' asked Bernard Mitchell. 'Do they come in?'

'They must,' replied the historian. 'You hand the ransom note to them, and let them get on with their investigation. If you don't bring them in, your sharehold-ers will want to know why. The police will certainly advise you not to pay the ransom.'

'How do we get round that?'

'The ransom note will give detailed

instructions. The money will be dropped in the phone kiosk at the corner of West Side and South Side, Wimbledon Common between two and three a.m. on a given day; and MIL will be ordered *not* to call in the police. But as law-abiding citizens you do so.'

'Won't that blow the whole affair?' asked Dyer, mystified.

'My dear man!' said Macalister pityingly. 'All that is for the benefit of the police. What really happens is you pack half a million in notes of reasonably small denomination — unmarked, needless to say — in a brown paper parcel and deposit it in the Piccadilly Branch of the National Westminster Bank. You then post the receipt to me at my Bloomsbury address. This gives me effective control of the money.'

'You still need a signature to get the money out?' said Archer.

'Of course. Whoever deposits the money will have to come with me when the parcel is recovered and sign for it. This is the great advantage of a friendly kidnap. No danger of the money falling into the wrong hands. On Drop-Day the police will be swarming all over Wimbledon Common with telescopes trained on the innocent phone box, but by then the money will have been deposited neatly and expeditiously miles away.'

'There'll be a helluva row with the police.'

'I don't suppose they'll like it much; but they can't do anything about it except curse you. You're not bound to act on police advice in a kidnapping case.'

'Can we have time to think it over?' asked Dyer.

Before the historian could answer, Archer broke in:

'No point, Maurice. We settle this one way or the other, here and now. Agreed, Bernard?'

'I agree; and I say we go along with what is proposed.'

'So do I. Maurice?'

'I don't see we've any alternative — if the kidnap scheme is foolproof.'

'It is,' said Macalister confidently. 'If you obey instructions. They're all in here.'

He handed the chairman a fat envelope.

'But just to make sure we're on the right wavelength: on Sunday morning you take the Rolls and drive towards Esher — for some plausible reason.'

Dyer thought for a moment.

'They've forgotten to deliver the newspapers?'

'It's happened before?'

'Yes. It often happens.'

'Good. You get as far as Green Lane, where you are held up. By two masked men in a hired van, I think. Swan National will do nicely, pleasantly conspicuous with their red, white and blue livery. They force you to park the Rolls in a side road, blindfold you and drive you off to an unknown destination.'

'May we ask where?' said Archer.

'Better keep it dark,' replied Macalister. 'That is, if we're going to play the game properly. You *might* have second thoughts and try to send the police after us.'

'Seems *we* trust you, but you don't have to trust us,' said Dyer bitterly. 'Of course, I can tell my wife?'

'Good God, no.'

'I'm afraid he's right, Maurice. If we are going through with this charade — and I take it we're now committed? — we must go the whole hog. Hard on Matilda, but there it is. If she's in the know she could give the whole show away. And it would make her part of the — the conspiracy.'

'May I suggest,' said Macalister, 'that an accidental fire might dispose of the corresponding papers in your archives? Whitehall's habit of doing everything in triplicate may mean the Treasury have a copy of the Supply papers. One day somebody else might put two and two together. Though it's most unlikely at this time of day. The killer document (sorry, unfortunate adjective) is the memorandum which I — ah — removed, and of which you now have the only copy. Nevertheless — '

'Point taken,' grunted Dyer.

'Before you go,' said Archer suddenly. 'One question. Since we are being very frank with each other. Did you have anything to do with the death of that young man at Kew? Or have you any information about it, which the police don't have?'

For the first time the historian seemed to be taken at a disadvantage. He allowed his briefcase to fall to the floor. He quickly recovered his composure, however, although for the moment there was no trace of a smile on his face.

'Would I turn up here if I *was* involved?'

He laughed, rather uncertainly it seemed to the others. Archer pressed the point.

'Murder's a short step from a half-million blackmail.'

'The murder surprised me — as it surprised everybody else at Kew. If I *am* guilty, you are accessories.'

'Only if we go along with your plan.'

Macalister laughed again. This time he seemed master of himself. He said:

'It's up to you. I'm happy to settle for fifty thousand from one of the Sundays — though I'd prefer your half million. Take it or leave it.'

Dyer looked at his colleagues, who nodded.

'We take it,' he said.

When Macalister had gone, Archer said:

'I don't like it — but we're stuck with it.'

'Is he the murderer?' asked Mitchell.

'Could he have gone through with this business if he is?'

'Might be a good actor,' replied Mitchell, 'with a terrific nerve.'

Dyer looked particularly unhappy. A worrying thought had struck him. He murmured:

'If he's killed once — '

'Not to worry, Maurice,' said Archer, quick to see what was troubling the chairman. 'You're quite safe. You're the goose that lays his golden egg.'

'After the egg's laid?'

'We become your insurance policy. For the record we believe he's not guilty. Of murder.'

'I hope we're right,' said Dyer gloomily.

'It would have been so much simpler, Maurice,' said Mitchell, 'if you'd read classics instead of history.'

The chairman was too deep in depression even to hear this observation.

10

So far Peter Plumb's efforts to record on film the police investigation of the Kew murder had been limited to shots inside and outside the Public Record Office, of the paternoster delivering its scholarly loads, discreet glimpses of the surveillance system (he didn't want to highlight Big Brother but had the wit to see that surveillance might play a part in the solution of the mystery), sequences of Inspector Robinson and Sergeant Tough going about their business, supplemented by a general selection of their nods, smiles and puzzled frowns to be cut into the documentary in due course. To this was added the half-minute on finding the murder weapon, and a colourful rostrum camera picture of the great map of Calais which the Princess had not been allowed to see.

At first the policemen were rather camera-shy, but they soon got used to their unaccustomed role and became happily oblivious of the BBC team.

Peter saw the ritual help sought by the police from Julian Hardcastle as his first real opportunity — the appearance of a major character in the drama. Before Hardcastle was formally questioned by Inspector Robinson the young man was allowed to brief him about the BBC's interest in the affair, which he did with some trepidation, since the scholar was under no obligation to co-operate. As it turned out, Hardcastle positively welcomed the idea of being filmed. He explained:

'I have the greatest respect for our police, despite the current widespread campaign to undermine them; but they like all of us can make mistakes. If they think I killed this man, whom I have never met, they *are* making a mistake. I have therefore no objection to appearing in your film. Indeed I am most happy to do so. Since I am innocent of this particular crime, the experience will be rewarding and cost me nothing.'

'In that case,' said Peter, highly

gratified, 'would you mind saying that all over again for the benefit of the camera?'

'Delighted,' said Hardcastle, and proceeded to do so. He did not include in his somewhat pompous scholarly statement for the film any suggestion that the free publicity would do no harm to the sales of his books.

Fortunately for the peace of mind of Robinson and especially Tough — for it was the sergeant's discovery of the erased entry in the surveillance record and his subsequent deductions that had put Hardcastle on the spot — they were not present at this preliminary filming session. When they did come face to face with their suspect, and the camera tucked away discreetly at the far end of the interview room at Kew Police Station, they were still confident that it was only a matter of time before they had a confession in their notebooks, and on film for the edification of the Great British Public.

Robinson had no hesitation in attacking right from the start:

'Mr Hardcastle, we have reason to

believe that you may be able to help us in our enquiries into the death of Kevin Wigmore in the Public Record Office on or about Wednesday 29 December last.'

Hardcastle said nothing. The inspector went on:

'The number of your PRO card is 31782?'

'I have nothing to say.'

'You sat at Table 8 H in the Reading Room at Kew on 20 December last?'

'No comment.'

The inspector exploded.

'These are questions of fact,' he cried. 'There's no point in denying them. It would help us if you were to admit them.'

Hardcastle grinned and said:

'I don't have to help you, Inspector.'

'You realize,' went on Robinson, 'that it can only lead to difficulty if you persist in this foolish attitude?'

'Difficulty for you, Inspector. Hardly for me.'

Robinson looked helplessly at his sergeant. They both knew well that Hardcastle was under no obligation to answer any of their questions; and they had no warrant for his arrest. They could of course arrest him without warrant on a murder charge, but at this stage Robinson was not prepared to go as far as that.

'Come outside a minute, Jim,' said the inspector. The pair left the interview room.

As soon as the door closed behind them Hardcastle whispered:

'You have a hand-held camera?'

'Yes,' answered Peter, wondering what was coming next.

'Loaded?'

'Yes,' said the cameraman.

'Can you run?'

It was the cameraman's turn to look surprised. He said:

'Every Saturday. Wing three-quarter for Blackheath's Fifth Fifteen.'

'That should do,' said Hardcastle. 'I was a centre in my time.'

'What's this all about?' asked Peter, but before Hardcastle could enlighten him Robinson and Tough had returned. As they sat down the scholar rose, winked at Peter and dashed from the room. He sped along the corridor and through the entrance hall and in a single bound cleared the steps down to the street. He was closely followed by the cameraman who had happily divined what was expected of him.

Hardcastle cannoned into a young constable coming up the steps and sent him sprawling on the pavement. He then turned left and, with the cameraman still within comfortable range, headed towards Kew Green and the main entrance to the Royal Botanic Gardens.

The few passers-by observed their progress with some interest but made no attempt to impede it. It was obvious that a film was being made, probably to advertise some third-rate product on TV. They were still unmoved when the young constable hove in sight, a bad third. The consensus was that his costume and make-up were substandard. He was in fact a pretty poor apology for a stage policeman unlikely to make it outside a provincial repertory company.

At the main gate to the Botanic Gardens Hardcastle wasted no time stumping up the thirty new pence admission fee. To the astonishment of the Royal Botanic Gardens constable posted there to relieve him of that sum he vaulted the turnstile and made his way, still at a good clip, along Broad Walk.

The deprived constable was about to abandon his post and give chase when the member of the Blackheath Rugby Club's Fifth Fifteen appeared on the scene and emulated his predecessor, rather less athletically, being hampered by his camera. A few seconds later the constable who had been bowled over at the police station arrived, shouted something incomprehensible to his Botanic fellow, vaulted the turnstile and disappeared along Broad Walk in the wake of the others.

At the end of the walk Hardcastle began to realize that he was neither as young nor as fit as he had once been, and decided it was time to bring his performance to an end. He sought sanctuary within the walls of the Orangery. He collapsed on a bench in front of a display, 'Portrait of a Tropical Forest', resisting with difficulty an impulse to hide in a nearby Roman sarcophagus. There he calmly awaited the arrival of the pursuit.

The cameraman and constable dead-heated, which made it possible for the former to get an excellent shot of the latter formally arresting Hardcastle and frog-marching him back to the police station, into the welcoming arms of a thoroughly bemused Inspector Robinson.

Within a few minutes the escaper was again seated on the inquisitorial chair he had so recently vacated, still breathing heavily, but looking very pleased with himself. Peter Plumb caught his eye and detected an unmistakable wink.

Robinson said:

'I understand from Constable March that when you left this building you deliberately knocked him over. Further, when he arrested you, you struck him in the eye. I have therefore no alternative but to charge you with assaulting a police officer. Anything you say may be taken down and used in evidence.'

'By all means, Inspector,' said Hardcastle. 'I do say that I am surprised. It is true I knocked the constable over. Sheer accident, I assure you, and I am very sorry. It was impossible to avoid him. But why an innocent citizen should be pursued and eventually tackled by a fourteen-stone policeman is beyond my comprehension. If my elbow caught him in the eye when he laid hands on me — again, it was a complete accident.'

'You may send for your solicitor, if you wish.'

'Thanks a lot,' said Hardcastle cheerfully, 'but I'm happy to leave myself in the hands of British justice. And I can't really afford a solicitor. Might be a different matter if I was guilty.'

When he had been removed to a cell to ponder his position Peter had a word with the inspector. He explained that in his preliminary interview with Hardcastle he had the clear impression the man was innocent.

'Then why the hell play games with us?' demanded the inspector angrily.

'I think I know,' replied Peter. 'If you're a struggling author — '

'Good God! You think we're being taken for a ride — as a sort of publicity stunt?'

'Something of the sort,' said Peter gently. 'Helping the police for a few minutes doesn't catch the headlines. Detention for twenty-four hours with murder hanging over your head is a better bet.'

'Good God!' said the inspector again. 'If you're right — what do we do now?'

'It's awkward,' put in Sergeant Tough. 'He could have left the station a free man, and there's no law saying he must leave at walking pace. And you can't blame March for going after him. Anybody would have done the same. But I can see defence counsel making a big thing of the honest citizen's wish to get as far away as possible from a police station as quickly as possible. If he *did* stick an elbow in March's eye it could be dressed up as a natural reflex action.'

Robinson groaned and said:

'If we throw him out without another interview, we're no forrarder. And as he's been arrested he's entitled to appear before the magistrates. Hell!'

'If I may make a suggestion,' said Peter. 'Keep him overnight, and try a few questions on him tomorrow. After the nationals have got him in their headlines it'll be a different story. He'll be eating out of your hands.'

★   ★   ★

In fact, the Press were much indebted to Hardcastle for his brief encounter with the police. The affair at Kew, which promised so much, had seemed to be petering out. The communiqué that a murder headquarters had been set up in Fort Ruskin, that the police were energetically pursuing their enquiries and following promising leads, didn't cut much ice. Julian Hardcastle's assistance to the authorities changed all that.

Although his name was by no means a household word he was not a nonentity; and it so much better when a public figure strays from the path of righteousness. His dramatic dash for freedom had been captured on film by a botanist visiting the gardens to photograph the desolate winter beauty of the weeping beeches flanking Broad Walk, and whose quick-witted enterprise earned him a small fortune from the media.

Next morning's Sunday papers went as near as the law of libel allowed to suggesting that Hardcastle *was* the murderer. They harked back to earlier scholarly murders, even dragging in one engineered by the Borgias, seeking to draw comparisons between those crimes and the Kew affair — not easy since the one thing generally agreed about the last was that there had never been anything like it.

Hardcastle's escapade was the lead story in BBC TV's evening news, unfortunately denied Peter Plumb's footage of the chase, which he successfully fought to reserve for his documentary. Like the Sundays, the BBC had to make do with the stills provided by the botanist photographer, thereby adding further to his windfall profits.

About noon on Sunday Hardcastle was escorted from his cell to the interview room where Robinson and Tough were waiting for him. He had seen the papers and their gratifying headlines, and although unshaven and unkempt was in cheerful mood, with the air of one who has just successfully accomplished a tricky mission. Before Robinson could speak, he took the floor:

'In answer to your questions, inspector: Yes, my PRO reader's card is 31782. It is graven on my heart, which make it easy to put into the computer. My number, not my heart. Yes, I sat at Table 8 H at Kew on 20 December last. We are creatures of habit. I always sit at 8 H — if nobody has got there first. I was there all day until the place closed, except for lunch and necessary visits to the loo. I think that brings us up to date. Any further questions?'

'Certainly,' said Robinson grimly. 'On that day you requisitioned Ministry of Supply file AVIA 1 333?'

Hardcastle seemed to be caught off balance. This was not a question he had expected. He replied:

'I did not.'

'And removed from it pages 100 to 120?'

'Good heavens, no! What's this all about?'

'In that case,' went on the inspector, playing his trump card, 'how do you account for this?'

He passed over a computer requisition slip dated 17 December recording that J. Hardcastle sitting at Table 8 H had ordered file AVIA 1 333. Hardcastle examined it carefully, and even held it up so that the camera at the end of the interview room might see it better over his shoulder.

Then he said easily:

'I think I begin to understand. Very ingenious! First, although I do use Ministry of Supply files in my research, I don't remember ever asking for this one. Second, the requisition slip does have my name, and reader and table numbers. When that information was fed into the computer it had to deliver the file to my place; but it was not delivered to me.'

The inspector found Hardcastle's confidence disconcerting. He looked to Tough the computer expert for support, but the sergeant was equally nonplussed. The scholar enjoyed their discomfiture. He went on:

'It's very simple. Wish I'd thought of it myself. I find out where another reader is sitting. Right? I memorize his reader's card number. How? I stand behind him in the queue waiting to use the computer terminal, and read off his number as it comes up on the screen.

'Later, when he's at lunch, I use his card number to requisition a file, which the computer obligingly sends to me, now sitting at his place. If I cut the file in small pieces the owner of the card number will get the blame. I gather that somebody *has* mutilated the file in question. I assure you it wasn't me.'

'You suggest another reader played a trick on you?'

'It could be a mistake, but I hardly think so. And if papers were actually taken from the file it looks pretty sinister. There's a perfectly good photocopying system. So why *remove* papers?'

'If someone *did* use your numbers in this way,' said the inspector, 'it could be any one of the readers there on the day?'

'Obviously. About two hundred of them, I suppose. Don't ask me which.

I've no idea, and I don't really care.'

'What about Mr Macalister?' suggested Tough.

Hardcastle roared with laughter.

'You've heard about that little episode? Revenge is sweet, eh? Hardly. Macalister is an unscholarly money-grubbing twit. And a coward to boot. He wouldn't risk his miserable career — and that's what pinching PRO papers would mean — to settle an old score. You'll have to look somewhere else. Among the other 199 possible starters.'

He turned to the camera and asked:

'Got all that OK? If not, I'm happy to provide take two. I assume I'm now free to leave, Inspector? Your accommodation is admirable, though perhaps not quite up to London club standards. I need a wash and brush-up.'

★   ★   ★

When Hardcastle had left the station, this time at a sedate walking pace, Robinson rounded on his sergeant more in sorrow than anger.

161

'Well, Jim? You've made a right cock-up of it this time!'

'He could be bluffing, sir,' replied Tough without much conviction.

'Bluffing, my backside! He knew he was on to a good thing and would make bloody fools of us. And I thought you were a computer buff! Could it happen like he said?'

'Yes; but it doesn't mean it did. It could be a double con. And we've made an even bigger cock-up by letting him go.'

'Damn all academics,' said the inspector with feeling.

'Suppose the two things are not connected?' suggested Tough.

'Pinching the papers, and the murder? They must be. Wigmore spots somebody taking the papers — not Hardcastle, if we believe his story — blackmails him and is duly got rid of. At any rate, Hardcastle confirms the papers must have contained something nasty. I suppose now you can read secret papers after only thirty years there must be lots of stuff people would like suppressed. The moles of thirty years ago, to start with. Suppose I was spying for the Russians in the 1950s? Somebody wrote a memorandum about me that wasn't taken seriously at the time. Wouldn't I like to tear it up before some journalistic spy-hunter gets hands on it and rushes me off to the Old Bailey?'

'If we knew what was stolen it would help,' said Tough. 'There may be a copy on another file.'

Robinson was pursuing his own line of thought.

'Somebody was trying to pin the theft on Hardcastle — '

'*Only* the theft,' interrupted Tough. 'Not the murder. I think that's important. When the papers were pinched nobody knew the murder was going to happen.'

'Unless it was part of a plan. Seems to me,' said the inspector frowning 'that the Macalister–Hardcastle fight puts Macalister in the clear. He wouldn't take the risk, knowing their row was public property. If the two things aren't connected, what do we get? Somebody — not Macalister — stole the papers, hoping to incriminate Hardcastle. Why, we don't know.'

'It's possible,' said Tough, 'that whoever

tried to land the theft on Hardcastle had no idea who he was. He just waited for somebody — anybody — who took a long lunch hour.'

'So somebody else killed Wigmore? Why, we don't know. Damn all academics,' said Robinson again, more vehemently. 'Give me the failed-O-level criminal every time. I need a drink. Come on!'

11

Sir Maurice Dyer's Saturday afternoon at the golf club, usually the highlight of his week, had been ruined by endless talk about the Kew murder, which seemed to have caught everybody's imagination. Even the pre-lunch gin session, which he shared with a member of parliament, an oil executive, and a High Court judge, and which was as a rule devoted exclusively to racing and, depending on the season, rugby or cricket, with perhaps a few moments devoted to the latest national crisis, could talk of nothing else.

Dyer found himself listening to his friends with a split mind: half considering what they were saying from their position of ignorance, half formulating his own contribution (which he refrained from making) in the light of his special knowledge, if not of the murder, at least of events which might disastrously be associated with it.

'In my opinion,' said the High Court judge, after his third pink gin, 'the computer is the guilty party. It was bound to happen sooner or later. Frankenstein's monster rules OK. If it appears before me I shall sentence it to life defusement.'

'You're very silent, Maurice,' said the oil executive. 'Not interested in the bizarre crimes of our day? How do *you* explain the inexplicable mystery?'

'Haven't a clue,' replied Dyer hastily, wishing they would change the subject. 'In fact, I don't know anything about the case.'

This was a mistake, for the High Court judge, capable of effortless and comprehensive summing-up, even in his sleep, devoted the remaining few minutes before they went in to lunch to a lucid exposition of the facts — an admirable performance in strange contrast to his standard performance on the golf-course.

Dyer's own performance that afternoon was marred by numerous shanks and even an air shot; and his side handsomely lost the 50 pence, the modest inverted snob sum for which the four regularly played. The round completed, he detached himself after only one Scotch, an unwonted act of abstinence which caused further adverse comment from his companions after he had gone.

As he drove home he speculated about the chances that he and his fellow directors might take the place of the computer in the dock before his friend the judge; and he derived little comfort from the thought that judges were usually discouraged from trying their friends and fellow club members.

He poured his wife her evening glass of sherry and himself a king-size Scotch. Lady Dyer had long since become resigned to the Saturday ritual, which denied her the pleasure of her husband's company for most of the day. Many years earlier she had taken up golf in self-defence, but before long reluctantly accepted that nature had not intended her to be a golfer. Fortunately she was a resourceful woman and found other pastimes to occupy her Saturdays.

Dyer had a long pull at his Scotch

before switching on the BBC TV evening news.

Five minutes later he was on the telephone to Gilbert Archer.

'Seen the news? No? Extraordinary thing. That chap Hardcastle — the fellow you thought would make a good job of our history, and nearly finished off our historian — was being questioned by the police about the murder at Kew. Escaped from the police station, but was caught again in Kew Gardens. In the Orangery, of all places. They say he's helping the police again — so it looks as if *our* man is in the clear.'

'I don't know that we want to talk about this on the phone,' said Archer. '*Your* man — ' he lingered maliciously on the pronoun — 'may or may not be responsible for *that* crime, but you will not have forgotten that he has another — still pretty serious — in the pipeline.'

'I have *not* forgotten,' replied Dyer coldly. 'And I'm not particularly looking forward to tomorrow. I hope that you will not forget — or muck up — your part.'

'I'm sorry, Maurice. Not to worry. We'll

look after things at this end. Best of luck.'

Dyer was left somewhat deflated. The shadow of murder — of accessory to murder — might have been lifted, but the conspiracy to be kidnapped still remained. *That* charade still had to be acted out, with him in the starring role. He adjourned to the decanter and helped himself to another king-size Scotch, fully conscious of the aura of disapproval emanating from his spouse. He wondered how she would react to the events of tomorrow.

At eight next morning, while Lady Dyer was still asleep, he left the house by the front door, where the Sunday newspapers were already lying. Since the agreed reason for his early morning trip was to collect papers which the newsagent had forgotten to deliver, it would hardly do to leave them there. As he gathered them up he saw that all the front pages were devoted to Hardcastle's exploit in Kew Gardens and his subsequent detention by the police. Their implication was that he was the Kew murderer was comforting, since it followed that Macalister must be innocent.

He drove slowly along Sandy Lane towards Esher and as instructed turned into Green Lane. There was no sign of the promised Swan National van and he began to think something must have gone wrong; but a quarter of a mile further on Macalister emerged from behind a rhododendron bush, his gleaming locks concealed in a hooded anorak, and flagged him down. He greeted him cheerfully and explained:

'Sorry about the van. I found that to hire it meant producing my driving licence. That might have led to later complications. I should have thought the procedures through more carefully.'

So you should, thought Dyer. If his kidnapper was capable of making an elementary mistake . . .

'My Jag is parked just off the road. Much more comfortable than a van.'

'Where are we going?'

'To a delightful place on the west coast of Scotland — the back o' beyond. We shan't be disturbed — I've spent holidays there and know the place well. Not the best time for a trip to Scotland, but beggars can't be choosers. The Gulf Stream does keep it reasonably warm even now. If it were summer I could offer you shooting, fishing and deer stalking. Still, we can't have everything in this life.'

He seemed to be genuinely distressed that circumstances prevented him from being the perfect host.

'We couldn't have gone by rail?' said Dyer as he settled into the passenger seat and fastened his seat-belt. 'I hate long road journeys.'

'I agree. Rail is much to be preferred, but you would be certain to be spotted. You *are* a national figure, after all. And if you were seen in a comfortable first-class carriage, it would be bad for all of us.'

That was true, thought Dyer. And after this business he would no doubt be an international figure. At least when this final hurdle was taken the nightmare of the past weeks would vanish. Normal life would be resumed.

As the Jag drove away he took a last

loving look at the Rolls, his pride and joy. Then he yelled:

'Just a minute!'

Macalister gave him a nasty look, fearing that he was about to have second thoughts about the whole enterprise.

'The newspapers!'

'What about the newspapers?'

'The idea was that I had gone to the newsagents to collect them. They were all on the doorstep when I left, so I brought them with me. They're in the car — we'd better take them with us. Otherwise my story will very likely be blown.'

Macalister frowned and went back for the papers.

'I suppose you're right,' he admitted, 'but we may have to change the story. Why were there no papers? Had they blown away? There's no wind. Could have been stolen, I suppose. You saw the headlines? My colleague Hardcastle seems to be in some trouble with the police.'

'I saw them,' replied Dyer, as he steeled himself for the marathon drive. 'Very interesting.'

* * *

Next morning the national press had an embarrassment of riches. Further stories about the questioning of Hardcastle in connection with the most sensational murder of the decade rubbed shoulders with speculation about the disappearance of one of the country's leading tycoons.

A neighbour had recognized the abandoned Rolls and telephoned Lady Dyer to say where it was standing. At first she thought her husband had gone for an early morning walk, although he was not keen on walking, except round a golf-course; and then, realizing that the Sunday papers had not been delivered, she thought he had gone to fetch them. When the newsagent swore he *had* delivered them, Lady Dyer became alarmed and called the police, after checking with the rest of the MIL board that they didn't know where Dyer had gone. It was with difficulty that Gilbert Archer disclaimed all knowledge of the chairman's whereabouts, for Lady Dyer was beside herself with anxiety; but he had no doubt that it would be foolish to take any chances at this stage of the game.

The police quickly established that Dyer was not the victim of a road accident, nor was there reason to think he might be wandering round in a state of amnesia. His colleagues dismissed any idea that he might have gone abroad in connection with some secret business deal. In any case his passport was still in a drawer in his desk. There seemed little doubt that he had been abducted.

Speculation ended the following morning when Gilbert Archer told the police he had received a letter from the kidnappers. Dyer was being held to ransom, and for half a million pounds he would be returned safe and sound. Instructions about handing the money over would follow later; but if MIL valued their chairman's life they must on no account call in the police. Inspector Wainwright of Scotland Yard, in charge of the case, complimented Archer on his public spirit in defying the kidnappers' instructions in spite of the possible consequences for the chairman.

The communication received by MIL was made up of single letters cut from the *Daily Express*, carefully stuck on A4 Croxley typing paper with ordinary PVA paste — all of which could be bought anywhere in the country. The franking showed that the letter had been posted in central London on Sunday. Various terrorist organizations immediately made half-hearted attempts to claim credit, but the police ruled them all out. There was no suggestion that Sir Maurice's life was being offered in return for the freedom of any prisoner, political or otherwise. It followed that the only possible motive was private financial gain.

The eager newspapers culled their files for the latest photographs of Dyer, and also printed the earliest — a stirring picture of the mountainous forward lumbering across the line in a Calcutta cup game at Twickenham to score his only try for England. Letters and phone calls flooded in from every county in Britain and several countries in Europe claiming that the missing industrialist had been seen. He appeared in Sydney, Australia, long before even Concorde could have carried him there. There were interviews with an anguished Lady Dyer who pleaded before the television cameras for the safe return of her husband. A consultant psychiatrist deduced from the ransom letter that the gang must include someone who had at least O-level English and a very steady hand, which did not materially reduce the suspect field.

Scotland Yard feared that although MIL appeared to be co-operating and laying all the meagre facts before them the firm might secretly try to get in touch with the kidnappers and pay up, no questions asked. As they went through the motions of sifting evidence and evolving theories they reminded Gilbert Archer that if the gang was to be brought to justice the police must be kept in the picture about any dealings the firm had with them. To which he replied that of course they would have the firm's full co-operation.

In saying this he passed the point of no return. When the second note arrived instructing that the money was to be dropped in the phone-box at South Side, Wimbledon Common, between 2 and 3 a.m. two days later Archer passed it on to the police without comment, but with considerable misgiving. Failure to co-operate with the police in a kidnap investigation was one thing. Deliberately to mislead them was another.

However, this did not deter him from carrying out MIL's part of the bargain. MIL's bank in the City produced half a million in notes without demur, the manager having read the headlines and having been told in confidence by Archer what was in the wind. Archer was surprised at the small space the money occupied. It was astonishing to think that even a multi-millionaire could carry his entire fortune round the world in a weekend case. The bank clerk who received the half million was manifestly bored by the transaction, assuming perhaps that the package contained family silver. The deputy chairman found this lack of interest comforting. It dispelled the feeling of guilt from which he suffered and suggested that to deposit half a million pounds in a shady kidnap deal was a run-of-the-mill affair not worth a second thought.

He accepted the safe custody receipt and escaped thankfully into Piccadilly where he posted the receipt to Macalister's address. There was now nothing to be done but await developments.

That evening the crumb of comfort which the inner cabinet of MIL had derived from the arrest of Hardcastle was instantly dissipated by the news of his release.

'Wonder if Maurice has heard?' Archer asked Bernard Mitchell. 'If so, how did he react?'

'Thinking he's in the hands of a murderer? Not too well, I fear.'

★   ★   ★

In fact, Dyer *had* heard the news of Hardcastle's release, apparently without a stain on his character.

The chairman and his kidnapper reached their destination on Sunday evening after a terrifying high-speed drive with only one stop for petrol. When they crossed the border they found the end of one of those rare Scottish winter days when the only purpose of the scattered fleecy cloud is to set off the pale blue of the sky. The sparkling waters of the mountain torrents, dappled greens and browns of the nearby hills and delicate purples of the more distant ranges were a joy to behold — viewed from the comfortable warmth of the car.

Their ultimate goal was a chalet, one of six built on his estate by an impoverished landlord helping to make ends meet. In summer all six would be taken, but at this time of year Macalister reckoned there would be no other visitors. The only sign of life in the last twenty miles of their journey was provided by herds of shaggy red Highland cattle which did not trouble to interrupt their grazing to watch the passing Jaguar, and a few deer venturing down from the higher slopes in search of food. Dyer had to admit it would be difficult to find a better place for their particular enterprise.

Macalister, who knew his way round the chalet from previous visits, soon had a blazing fire going. While Dyer walked up and down in the darkness outside to get the stiffness out of his limbs, he produced a tolerable meal from the tins he had brought, although both men were so famished that anything would have tasted cordon bleu. Dyer, having only the clothes he left home in that morning, was without pyjamas and toilet things. Macalister provided him with pyjamas and toothbrush, but forbade him to shave on the ground that when he was returned to civilization he must be seen to have been deprived of the amenities of polite society.

After breakfast next morning Macalister went off to Mallaig to lay in supplies. Before leaving he warned Dyer that he must take care not to be seen, although the chances that anybody would come within miles of the chalet were remote. To encourage him to remain inside, although there was little incentive to go out without arctic clothing, he drew his attention to the small library which the chalet boasted, consisting mainly of the works of John Buchan, and he also gave him a transistor radio.

While Macalister was still away a BBC Radio 2 news broadcast informed Dyer that Hardcastle had been released; and for the next hour he struggled to evaluate the new situation. He comforted himself with the thought that since Macalister was still a partner in crime he was unlikely to harm him; but if he was guilty of murder their conspiracy now involved them all in that crime. On the other hand there was no need to worry about the death penalty. In these tolerant days there was little difference between the reward for murder and that for a major conspiracy not involving murder.

When Dyer realized that he might be the guest of a murderer he was at first tempted to bolt. It would have been easy enough to walk the ten miles to Mallaig. However, reason prevailed. The game must be played out in his own interest as well as MIL's.

Macalister returned laden with groceries, in cheerful mood. As he carried the cartons from the car Dyer asked:

'You heard? About Hardcastle?'

'Yes. On the car radio. I'm afraid Mallaig's cellars are not up to much. At least I've got some Chivas Regal.'

'If it wasn't Hardcastle, who was it?'

'No idea. In any case, it could still be Hardcastle. He may have been released while the police try to find more evidence.'

He seemed anxious to change the subject.

'I phoned Gilbert Archer. He says he's kept your part of the bargain.'

'I'm free to go?'

'Hardly. We need a bit more artistic verisimilitude.'

'Meaning?'

'It would look a bit odd if you reappear after one day, ransom paid and all the rest of it. I agreed three days with Archer. He saw the point.'

Dyer groaned.

'Three days of John Buchan — and Radio 2!'

'It's all in a good cause,' replied Macalister soothingly. 'I got a nice salmon in Mallaig, and some first-rate Aberdeen-shire beef. And I'm a pretty decent cook, although I say it myself.'

'Where do I go — when I *do* go?'

'We drive to Glencoe.'

'*Another* road journey?'

'Only three hours. There must be no connection with this place, so you make your reappearance somewhere else.'

'Why Glencoe?'

'We can get there easily from here. There's an old shepherd's hut on one of the Three Sisters. Well off the beaten track. I once camped near it. You've been held there — for four days remember — by men who disguised their voices, you think. You were blindfolded when they held you up, so there's little you can tell the police. You shelter in the hut till dawn — the men said if you left before then you stood a good chance of getting a bullet in your head. Then you walk down to the main road and thumb a lift. Suitably distrait and dishevelled.'

'That won't be difficult,' said Dyer bitterly. 'Very appropriate — Glencoe. Scene of a shameful act of treachery.'

Macalister laughed.'

'Good point. I'd forgotten you read history. You should have no difficulty in getting a lift — even at this time of year. There's plenty of traffic in the main road. Now, I suggest you start with *The Thirty-nine Steps*, while I get lunch.'

At 2 a.m. three days later they set out for Glencoe. In addition to the excellent meals provided by his host Dyer had worked his way through *The Thirty-nine Steps, Huntingtower* and two-thirds of *John Macnab*. A request to take the last with him to discover whether *John Macnab* won the day was instantly vetoed. There must be no clue to his recent whereabouts.

They arrived about 5 a.m. when Dyer was unceremoniously dumped on the lower slopes of the middle of the Three Sisters. Macalister had driven up as far as he dared — the Jaguar was not designed for a boulder-strewn track.

'You'll find the hut on the right-hand side about a quarter of a mile further on. Should be no difficulty in spotting it. Stay there till it's light, then come down to the main road. Sorry to leave you like this, but it's the only way. I'm sure you understand.'

'What happens to *you* now?'

'I return to the chalet where I'll lie low for a week or two continuing to enjoy my winter break. Then back to London to collect the cash at your convenience.'

Macalister turned the car with difficulty on the narrow track and then suddenly jumped out with a yell.

'I'm getting forgetful in my old age. What did you live on for four days in your hut?'

He opened the boot and brought out a plastic container.

'You'll find four empty Spam tins and eight empty beer cans in this. All carefully wiped clean of fingerprints — so only yours will be found on them. A Spartan diet, but enough to keep body and soul together. *Au revoir.*'

Dyer watched the Jaguar snake down the hill until it disappeared, and then started his slow progress up to the shepherd's hut. The half moon reflected in the torrents on either side gave him just enough light to steer a safe course. When he reached the hut he found it hardly worthy of the name. The door had fallen off and the wind, which had become stronger and colder as he ascended, whistled through cracks in the walls. A hardy young shepherd with a well-filled flask might survive there, not an elderly business man.

He carefully handled all the tins of his Barmecide feasts and dropped them in a corner. Then after ten minutes of misery he decided there was nothing for it but to set off for the main road and hope to reach it before he froze to death. So well had he absorbed his cover story that he found himself wondering for a moment if he would get a bullet in the head for disobeying orders.

12

'Seen the newspapers, sir?' asked Sergeant Tough as Robinson came into their room in the PRO. 'This kidnap affair?'

'Enough on our plate without worrying about other people's kidnaps. What's biting you, Jim?'

'Chap kidnapped is Sir Maurice Dyer.'

'So what?'

'Chairman of MIL.'

'Well?'

'Macalister's writing the history of MIL.'

'Think there's a connection? Coincidence, my boy. When you hear a new name or learn something new chances are that within a couple of days you'll come across it again. Now, if the file the papers were pinched from had been an MIL file — '

He was interrupted by a knock at the door.

'The expert from the Cabinet Office

Historical Section,' explained Tough. 'I thought you'd better hear the story straight from the horse's mouth.'

The staid inspector with difficulty restrained a guffaw as their visitor came in, for his sergeant's last words could hardly have been more — or less — felicitous. Miss Jennifer Sproat had the most equine features he had ever seen — high forehead, a long thin lined face terminating in a massive jaw. Her prominent teeth positively begged expert assessment of her age. Even her walk suggested a mature mare desperately anxious to break into a trot; and when the eye reached her fetlocks it came as a surprise that she was not shod with racing plates but with stout brown brogues.

'Miss Sproat, sir,' said Tough. 'She's been looking into the question of these missing papers.'

The expert sat down at the table and produced the vandalized file. She proceeded to recite her findings in the manner of a lecturer who knows her subject so well that she need not listen to what she is saying.

'AVIA 1 333. Ministry of Supply file. 250 folios. Correspondence between the Ministry's Contracts Department acting on behalf of the War Office, and Ultra Special Alloys Limited. Second half 1944. Folios 100 to 120 are missing, and must have been removed after the file was deposited in the PRO.'

'Can you guess anything about the missing pages?' asked the inspector.

'*Folios*,' said Miss Sproat severely. 'I was coming to that. Folio 99 is a letter to the firm dated 25 August. Folio 121 is the reply dated 27 August. You see the significance?'

'No,' admitted Robinson, still trying to fathom the difference between a folio and a page.

'It suggests that the missing folios were not part of the correspondence but a self-contained memorandum. Otherwise the reply to the earlier letter would be folio 100. That must be obvious.'

'Any hope of finding a copy of the missing — folios, on another file?'

'I think not — though one can't be certain. Because of the storage problem we try to keep only one set of papers. Which is why it is so important that papers reaching the PRO should be properly looked after. Of course, it's possible that the firm — Ultra Special Alloys — kept their files. You might try them.'

'Forty years is a long time,' observed the inspector.

'Some firms take a pride in their history,' replied Miss Sproat. 'Especially MIL. In fact, they have just commissioned their official history.'

'MIL?' chorused the two policemen.

'Of course.'

'But we were talking about Ultra Special Alloys.'

'USA Limited were a wholly owned subsidiary of MIL at the time of World War II. The became part of the main company in a post-war reorganization. Thought everybody knew that. Now, if that's all . . . ?'

Miss Sproat seized her brief-case and positively cantered from the room.

'Thought everybody knew that,' mimicked Tough when the door was safely closed. 'Well, I didn't; but you see — '

'I see,' said Robinson glumly. 'There *is* an MIL connection. You were right. Accidentally, no doubt. The MIL historian was there on the day. The papers stolen were USA which is MIL. But that's as far as I'm willing to go. I'm damned if I'm going out on another limb until I'm certain there's nobody with a chain-saw behind me. But — all right. Let's have another talk with Macalister.'

This was easier said than done. He was nowhere to be found in the PRO. A telephone call to his Oxford College produced the answer that he was in London. When Tough called in person at his Bloomsbury bedsitter there was no sign of him, nor did his immediate neighbours have any idea about his whereabouts. He usually spent the week-end there but not every weekend. Somebody was pretty sure they'd seen him on the previous Saturday, but not on the Sunday.

★   ★   ★

While they waited for Alistair Macalister to materialize again and Robinson and Tough followed up Miss Ernestine Dudley's vague suspicions that something odd might have transpired between Richard Bodley and Michael Carrington.

Bodley for his part continued to speculate about Carrington's sudden volte-face. As he pedalled the seven miles to Kew on this January day — springlike and totally unseasonable — he asked himself for the hundredth time what had gone wrong? Carrington was still working on his gambling papers, apparently making reasonable headway, in spite of his suggestion that they were more than one man could tackle — a verdict which Bodley readily confirmed from his brief experience of them.

And why gambling? It was difficult to believe that Carrington was suddenly thirsting for scholarly knowledge of the sixteenth century. Maybe he thought he would stumble on some long-forgotten truth that would make twentieth-century gambling foolproof. That was the most plausible explanation Bodley could think of — and it might also explain why he had so suddenly dispensed with his services. He had stumbled on something in the papers which he didn't want to share, *some* form of philosopher's stone, not necessarily connected with gambling.

On his arrival in the PRO Bodley was summoned by Robinson.

'I didn't think Miss Dudley would pass all that on,' he said in some surprise when the inspector asked about his relationship with Carrington. 'It can't have anything to do with the murder — if that's what you're suggesting?'

'You never know,' replied Robinson.

'Of course, I was surprised when Mr Carrington said he no longer needed me — after he had been so insistent that I should join him.'

'You've no idea why he changed his mind?'

'None at all; but as I say none of this can have anything to do with the murder. If you think of Mr Carrington's career — '

'Yes?' said the inspector as Bodley paused.

'He was — at least we *think* he was

— in the Secret Intelligence Service. M.I.6, you know.'

'I know,' replied Robinson, showing great toleration. 'Which puts him above suspicion?'

'Well, doesn't it?'

The inspector didn't answer. Instead, he asked:

'What about this burglary of yours. It seems to have been very convenient?'

'Convenient?' Bodley echoed in surprise.

'For Mr Carrington, I mean.'

'I don't understand,' said Bodley.

'According to Miss Dudley, Carrington had been badgering you to join forces with him here, but you refused. Then came the burglary, and you had to join him — for financial reasons?'

'That's right. You're not suggesting that Mr Carrington *organized* the burglary — for his own purposes?'

'Think of the sequence of events. He wants your help. He knows your insurance has lapsed, and that if you lose all your belongings you'll be in a mess.'

'Then why throw me overboard within

a matter of weeks?'

'That I can't explain,' admitted Robinson. 'I hoped you might have some idea.'

'I wish I had.'

'Perhaps Carrington will be able to help us. I'd be grateful if in the meantime you'd keep this conversation to yourself, Mr Bodley.'

When the inspector later gave an account of his meeting with Bodley to Sergeant Tough, he added:

'Before we talk to Carrington, we'd better find out a little about his antecedents. Bodley only *thought* he might have been SIS. Pretending to have been a secret agent could cover a multitude of careers. There's no need to give chapter and verse about what you were really doing. And if people think you *were* in the secret service they're usually too polite to quiz you about it.'

'If you'd been doing a ten-year stretch in Dartmoor it would be useful cover?'

'Yes.'

'SIS may not be too willing to talk about an ex-employee.'

'It'll be a different story if he's

masquerading as an ex-employee. We can but try.'

Robinson seized the telephone and in a few moments was conducting a cryptic conversation with a friend in the Special Branch, as a result of which he and Sergeant Tough found themselves later in the day in the presence of an amiable faceless individual in a secret building in an obscure part of the capital.

The faceless individual listened to the inspector's account with the greatest attention. At the end Robinson said:

'All we want to know is, was he one of yours? And do you know anything about his activities in retirement?'

'For your confidential information, the answer to your first question is yes; but the less said about that the better.'

'Understood.'

'About his retirement — perfectly normal, so far as we're concerned. Of course, if you come across anything odd, we'd like to know.'

'So much for the ten-year stretch in Dartmoor,' observed Robinson as they returned to Kew. 'I suppose all we can do now is listen politely to anything Carrington wishes to say.'

That proved to be very little. The inspector, who did not reveal that he had been in touch with the former agent's employers, gave a brief résumé of his interviews with Miss Dudley and Richard Bodley, leaving the impression that the police had read a good deal more into them than was the case.

Carrington listened patiently, and then said:

'The facts are pretty well as you say, Inspector. I have always hankered after historical research, and when I started off here I found the going tough. That was why I asked Bodley to lend me a hand. Then I found I'd bitten off more than I could handle financially, and decided I'd have to do without an assistant. It's slowed up my work, but that doesn't matter as it's only a hobby.'

'Thanks very much.'

'I suppose I shouldn't ask — but are you making progress?'

'It's not easy,' replied the inspector, feeling that he could be more open with

Carrington in view of his background.

'I'm sorry I can't be of more help, Inspector, but I wasn't here that afternoon.'

'Another dead end,' grumbled Robinson when Carrington had gone. 'What d'ye think, Jim?'

'Their row — if there *was* a row — can't have anything to do with Wigmore; and as Carrington says he wasn't even here. But there was one thing in what he said.'

'Yes?'

'He said he found the going tough *after* he started work here; but in fact he was trying to get Bodley to work with him long *before* he began his research. Why?'

'Slip of the tongue, I expect; and anyhow I don't see the significance. Meantime, let's find out if Macalister has come to roost anywhere.'

★ ★ ★

The two-mile walk down to the main road was a nightmare. Dyer would never have believed that such misery was possible, or that human spirit could endure it. The moon was now hidden by storm clouds which emptied themselves mercilessly into the driving wind. More than once he nearly stumbled off the track into a cataract that would have swept him disastrously down the mountainside. He had almost reached the point where it would be easier to lie down and leave things to nature when he saw that the main road was a mere hundred yards ahead. An articulated lorry swept past and disappeared in a cloud of spray before he could flag it; but not far behind was a private car.

He was in luck, for it was driven by an Edinburgh journalist on his way to report some convention in Inverness. When Archibald Gauld realized that the figure staggering towards him through the heather and wildly gesticulating was not a Sassenach suffering from a hangover, but the principal news story of the week, he sensibly forgot about his convention. He drove Dyer back to Edinburgh as quick as his Maestro would take him, treating his passenger with even greater solicitude than he would have lavished on the Loch Ness Monster or the Abominable Snowman.

As they drove he extracted Dyer's story. By the end of the journey he had a sizzling exclusive, illustrated with a photograph of the kidnap victim stumbling through the peat bog — one of the conditions of his agreement to take him back to civilization.

Although still suffering from the cumulative effect of recent events, and the perishing cold, Dyer saw that it was a stupendous stroke of luck to fall in with a journalist who had actually seen him stagger from his presumed place of captivity, and whose story would establish the fact of the kidnapping beyond all doubt.

That story, carefully memorized by Archibald Gauld, was that he had been held up by two masked men, blindfolded and driven to Glencoe, where he had been kept ever since. Had his captors discussed the ransom? No, they had hardly spoken at all. The sum asked was half a million pounds? Good heavens, surely MIL hadn't paid up? Gauld could not enlighten him on that, but presumed they must have done as he was now a free man. Where were the kidnappers now? Dyer explained they had left by car some hours earlier. It had taken him some time to untie himself, and they must be miles away by now. Had they treated him well? He had no real complaint, except that the diet of Spam had become rather monotonous.

By the time they reached Edinburgh the journalist had milked him dry. Gauld escaped to his office to write up the story, having first cleverly dropped Dyer at a tiny police station in the outskirts of the city where the sergeant in charge was one of the few people in the country unaware that the chairman of MIL had been kidnapped, and spent a frustrating hour taking a detailed statement. This enabled the resourceful Gauld to get his account on to the wire long before his confrères in TV, radio and the Press knew that Dyer had been returned to the fold and descended on him like a swarm of locusts.

Finally, after an ordeal almost as trying as his spell as a kidnap victim, Dyer was allowed to catch the night express from Edinburgh Waverley to King's Cross.

★   ★   ★

Meanwhile Archer and Mitchell in London had been on tenterhooks. Their last contact had been when Macalister telephoned from Mallaig for confirmation that the half million had been safely deposited, and had explained that Dyer would have to wait three more days before being released.

Thus the other two members of MIL's inner cabinet knew that their chairman had safely reached his destination. They could only wait, and hope that the rest of the plan would be plain sailing. On the day scheduled for the return of Dyer they were still waiting and hoping. Both kept transistor radios on their desks waiting for a news flash. None came.

There was still no news when they drove to the Gresham Club for lunch.

'He *must* be free by now,' said Mitchell

in exasperation. 'Unless something unpleasant has happened.'

'Such as?' asked Archer.

'I'd rather not think.'

'It's possible,' said Archer, 'that Maurice heard about Hardcastle's innocence, and panicked because he thought he himself might be next on Macalister's list.'

'If we don't hear by this evening,' said Mitchell. 'I suggest — '

As they passed the tape machine in the club entrance hall it began to chatter. Archer stopped to have a look. He grabbed Mitchell's sleeve.

'It's OK!' he cried.

If the machine's chatter was to be believed, the chairman of MIL had been held in some remote part of Scotland, and had been freed by his kidnappers that morning. It was not known whether the ransom they had demanded had been paid. Sir Maurice Dyer had been well treated. He wanted his wife to know that although he had been shaken by his experiences, he was in good health.

'Thank God!' said Mitchell. 'This calls for a celebration.'

13

Sir Maurice Dyer's hope that his safe return would restore the affairs of Megalith Industries Limited — and incidentally his own — to the position they had enjoyed before he engaged Alistair Macalister survived exactly one week.

He had taken a few days off to recuperate: even if he had not felt in need of a break it was an essential part of the cover-up of the phoney kidnapping. His colleagues pointed out that if he went back to the office as if nothing had happened people, especially the police, might be tempted to think nothing *had* happened. Therefore he must continue to live the part of the injured kidnappee who had been lucky to escape with his life and was still suffering from shock.

The week's convalescence prescribed by Gilbert Archer and Bernard Mitchell was no more than enough. He had come back from Scotland with a horrible cold — hardly surprising in the circumstances — and he found himself being nursed by his wife with a tenderness he had not believed possible. But a week after his reappearance in Glencoe he was back at his desk in MIL House.

His first meeting, after his secretary had welcomed him with tearful emotion, comforting as it was evidence that at least one person accepted the charade as fact, was with Archer and Mitchell. He provided them with a blow-by-blow account of the horrors of his simulated captivity, adding a lengthy footnote summing up his feelings about his erstwhile protégé Macalister, to which Archer forebore to add *his* footnote on the theme 'We told you so!' His colleagues explained what the police had done about the kidnapping, in particular the major operation they mounted in response to the second note from the kidnappers.

A brown paper parcel, filled with wads of cut-up newspaper, each topped with a five pound note, was planted in the designated phone-box at the south-west corner of Wimbledon Common ten minutes before 2 a.m. Twenty-four plain-clothes men were deployed in the vicinity, some in private houses, others on the roofs of King's College School and the Hand-in-Hand. There cars were parked some distance away on the only escape routes — the Crooked Billet, West Side Common, and South Side Common, to give chase should the kidnappers attempt to make a getaway.

Nothing significant had happened until a quarter past three. The hopes of the invisible watchers were raised when a car drew up. The solitary occupant, revealed by a nearby street lamp to be in evening dress, entered the phone-box and, before the police could move, put through a call. He hung up, emerged without the parcel and drove off quickly down the Crooked Billet. Inspector Wainwright, in command of the operation, radioed the car lying in wait there to follow at a discreet distance and ordered the rest of his troops to remain in position.

Five minutes later a white police Rover

with lights blazing skidded noisily to a halt by the phone-box.'

'What the hell?' muttered Wainwright on his point of vantage on the school roof.

Two uniformed policemen got out of the car, gingerly opened the phone-box door and peered inside. One knelt down and appeared to apply his ear to the parcel.

'That's torn it,' said Wainwright, divining what had happened. 'OK, chaps,' he went on into his microphone. 'Thanks a lot. We can all go home now.'

His uniformed colleagues still investigating the parcel were astonished at the sight of two dozen shadowy figures, cold, stiff and bad-tempered, converging on them. They concluded that the 999 call reporting a suspect bomb must be a prelude to a human attack; but happily Wainwright was able to enlighten them before they summoned reinforcements.

Some members of the failed ambush were able to see the funny side of the night's events, but Inspector Wainwright was not among their number; and when two days later the news of Dyer's release came through he had a somewhat frigid interview with Gilbert Archer. Although he did not say so outright he made it clear he believed MIL had done a secret deal with the kidnappers — why should the chairman have been released if they had not? — and further that the Wimbledon Common ploy was part of it.

The media's efforts to find out what ransom had been paid, and how, were stalled by a consistent 'no comment' from the deputy chairman, which convinced everybody, including the police, that the money had been handed over. A group of dissident MIL shareholders campaigned for an extraordinary meeting of the company to elicit the facts but they failed to get the support they needed.

In his confrontation with Wainwright Archer refused to say anything about the ransom, as he was entitled to do; but his attitude left the inspector in no doubt that he and his men had been wasting their time and taxpayers' money. By storming from the deputy chairman's room Wainwright left *him* in no doubt what the police thought about MIL's intransigence.

Having brought the chairman up to date Archer said he wanted to mention two matters: the firm's history, and the fate of the USAL papers.

'The less said about the history the better, I think. If we announce we've scrapped it, people will ask why. It could be awkward.'

'Macalister is still working on it?'

'Officially, yes. For the time being. Then we quietly forget the whole thing.'

'What to do about the USAL papers?' asked Dyer.

'It's done,' replied Archer. 'By my own hand. For better or worse.'

'Without telling our archivist?'

'Of course.'

'She'll find out. At the annual stock-taking, for example.'

'By that time we may have a new archivist,' said Archer.

'I see,' said Dyer, thoughtfully. 'Isn't that a bit hard?'

'*Sauve qui peut*,' replied Archer. 'We can give her a good reference.'

'Alternatively,' said Dyer, 'she could be a useful ally. If questions are asked about the papers, I mean. I think we hold on to her for the time being.'

'What *did* you do with the papers, Gilbert?' asked Bernard Mitchell.

'My garden incinerator.'

'Was that wise? There's no garden rubbish at this time of year.'

'You've a criminal mind, Bernard.'

'Don't we all,' said Dyer.

★ ★ ★

The inner cabinet of MIL were unaware that as they were burying the whole sorry affair, Robinson and Tough were working hard to exhume it. They had made formal application to the company secretary for permission to examine MIL's wartime papers. That officer had been surprised by the request. Commercial and economic historians did from time to time seek access to the firm's records; but this was the first request from the police. He saw no reason to refuse it, or even refer it to the board. In any case, the police could

210

no doubt compel the company to disgorge anything they wanted.

Tough found himself ascending to the tenth floor of MIL House on the express elevator which left the stomach several floors behind. He was received rather suspiciously by Miss Penelope Warner, the company archivist, but she soon warmed to his charm. A slim brunette in her early thirties, with provocative dark brown eyes, she was cast in a very different mould from Miss Sproat. Nevertheless, the sergeant sensed an underlying hardness in her manner which might predominate before many years had passed, perhaps the inevitable consequence of submersion in dry-as-dust papers six hours a day.

She explained she was authorized to produce any wartime records Tough wanted. The inspection of later company papers would have to be referred to the company secretary since they might contain confidential material. The sergeant said he was interested only in USAL records.

'USAL? No problem. They're on the

floor below. I'll tell the boy to bring them up.'

She was clearly dying to know why the police were interested, but was too well trained to ask.

Tough waited patiently for ten minutes, glancing at the latest issue of the glossy *MIL News Letter* lavishly illustrated with photographs of dams, bridges and hydro-electric schemes under construction, mammoth production lines, rubber, tea and coconut estates, mines working every known ore, and above all the faces of multi-coloured employees scattered between the frozen wastes of Kapuskasing in the Arctic and the South Island of New Zealand, all grinning broadly as if their next week's pay depended on it. Tough sensed that the attractive brunette's eye was examining him, not as a policeman, but as a man. Uncomfortable, but gratifying to one approaching middle age. The phone rang.

'Nonsense!' she said sharply into the instrument. 'Of course they're there. You can't have looked properly. I'll come down.'

She contrived in the last three words to convey the idea of immense sacrifice. Ten minutes later she returned, almost in a state of shock.

'I simply don't understand it. We can't lay our hands on *any* of the USAL papers. We had a weeding exercise recently and destroyed a lot of stuff of no interest. To save space, you know. But not the USAL files, unless they got in by mistake. In which case I'll be in trouble! I'll have to make a thorough search, Sergeant, and get in touch with you.'

Tough thanked her and departed, his head in a whirl not entirely due to the supersonic descent to the ground floor. He reported progress to Robinson in some excitement

'Where does this take us?' said the inspector. 'Fact: Wigmore sees somebody pinch MIL wartime papers, blackmails him and is killed by him. Right?'

'Right!' responded Tough dutifully.

'Fact: the killer tried to frame Hardcastle, so Hardcastle can't be the killer. Right?'

'Right!'

'Theory: Macalister would be a bloody fool to frame Hardcastle when it was known they hated each other. Right?'

'He may be a bloody fool.'

'Fact: Macalister had a foot in both PRO papers and MIL's own papers. Right?'

'Right!'

'Fact: twenty pages — '

'Folios.'

' — of public documents are stolen from USAL/MIL file in the PRO. All the USAL papers disappear from MIL House. Macalister has access to both sets of records. Right?'

'Right!'

'Fact: Macalister was in the PRO at both material times — when Hardcastle was set up, and when Wigmore was killed. Right?'

'Right!'

'Therefore — '

'Therefore the sooner we lay hands on Macalister the better.'

'Right! But first let's have a go at his boss.'

'Scotland Yard?' said Sir Maurice Dyer in considerable apprehension when his secretary told him the police wanted to see him. 'Thought we'd finished with them?'

'Not Scotland Yard, sir. It's Inspector Robinson and — ' there was a pause while Miss Grigg established identity of the second policeman — 'Sergeant Tough.'

'Send them in.'

There was no alternative, thought Dyer. If the police wanted to see him, see him they would. But why did they want to see him? And why these policemen?

'Inspector Robinson, sir,' said Inspector Robinson. 'This is Sergeant Tough. First, we must commiserate with you on your recent experiences. Must have been a great ordeal.'

'Unpleasant,' agreed Dyer. 'But it's water over the dam now.'

'We want to ask you about something else, however. We're investigating the murder of Kevin Wigmore in the Public Record Office at Kew. Last December. I expect you read about it?'

'I did. Extraordinary affair. How can I help?'

He thought furiously, wishing he could ask for Gilbert Archer to be present, if only for moral support — but that wouldn't do. There must be no hint that there was anything to worry about. He had to fight his way out of this on his own.

'We understand,' went on Robinson, 'that you recently commissioned a history of your firm.'

'That is so. Last year. To mark our two hundredth anniversary. The project had a good deal of publicity at the time.'

'Some of it unwelcome?'

Sir Maurice Dyer laughed.

'The fracas at our launching party? That was rather tiresome, but they say all publicity is good. You later arrested one of the contestants — in connection with the Kew murder?'

'We *questioned* Mr Hardcastle,' said the inspector. 'And we would now like to question Mr Macalister. Only we can't find him.'

'He commutes between Oxford and

Bloomsbury,' said Dyer.

'We tried both addresses, without success.'

'I suppose he could be on holiday. It's a good time to get out of this country. I really don't know. Perhaps our personnel division can help.'

'We want to question him about the removal of papers from the Public Record Office.'

'What does that mean?'

'It means theft, sir.'

'You think he was responsible?'

'We don't know, sir; but your related papers — those of Ultra Special Alloys — are also missing. There *may* be a connection.'

That this was a bombshell showed clearly on Dyer's face. The effect was not lost on the policemen.

'How on earth do you know our papers are missing? I've heard nothing about it. Did Macalister remove them too?'

'Your company secretary gave us permission to look at them; but they can't be found. Any of them. And as Macalister had access to them — it does seem to link up with the PRO theft.'

'Most extraordinary! Why should he want to *steal* our records? He had completely free access to them for the purposes of his work. You must certainly get hold of him as quickly as possible — and we will give you all the help we can. I'll get Miss Grigg to take you to Mr Muir of our personnel division.'

As Robinson and Tough were leaving, Miss Warner suddenly appeared in the chairman's outer office. She said, addressing Tough:

'I heard you were with the chairman. About these papers. I've drawn a blank. I think they've been stolen.'

'We've just been talking about them, Miss Warner,' said Dyer. 'The police are inclined to agree with you — and they think they know who might have taken them. On the other hand, I remembered authorizing the destruction of some old records a few months ago. Could the USAL files have found their way into that exercise?'

The archivist frowned and thought for a moment.

'It *is* possible, Sir Maurice. We did have a wholesale clearance. Nothing of any real interest — and I don't remember the USAL papers.'

'Well, there you are, gentlemen. Sorry we can't be of any more help for the moment.'

Mr Muir of Personnel Division was charming, but quite unable to throw light on the whereabouts of Macalister. He explained that while the historian was subject to the firm's staff regulations, like everybody else, in the nature of things he could not be expected to sign in and sign out like the rank and file. In any case, much of his work was done at Kew and in Bloomsbury.

'Well,' said Robinson, as they left MIL House. 'They seem to think Macalister could have pinched both the Kew and the USAL papers; but they can't give any reason why.'

'When we interviewed Macalister,' said Tough, 'he said something about the commercial value of old records. For example, the Foreign Office files on the Suez war would be worth their weight in gold to a historian.'

'Or to the Sunday papers,' added Robinson. 'But there's not much sex appeal of that sort in a firm's records.'

'Commercial secrets?' suggested Tough.

'Not worth a great deal after forty years. No, there's something else we don't understand.'

★   ★   ★

Later Dyer reported the events of the afternoon to Archer and Mitchell. He summed up:

'The police think Macalister took that memorandum from the PRO. They know our USAL files are missing, and they suspect he may have taken them too.'

'How do they know about the USAL files?' demanded Archer angrily.

'They asked to examine them in the ordinary way, and Jarvis in the ordinary way gave his approval.'

'Damn!' said Archer. 'We should have thought of that.'

'No harm done, I don't think. As the police were leaving Miss Warner came in to say the papers were stolen. I hinted that they might have been destroyed along with other papers, and she, bless her, did not rule out that idea.'

'What does she really think?'

'I don't know, but it'll do no harm to keep in touch with her thinking from now on. Incidentally, the police are trying hard to get hold of Macalister.'

'When does he get back?'

'The idea was he'd lie low for a week or two, to let things simmer down generally. When the coast is clear he'll contact us to collect the cash.'

'With the police on his tail? It's going to be tricky.'

'Better leave the money where it is, say for a couple of months. If Macalister will agree.'

'What worries me,' said Mitchell, 'is the murder. Which as I understand it, Maurice, the police didn't mention. It looks more and more as if they're really after him for murder; and if he's involved, so are we. If we *know* the ransom money is in effect the proceeds of murder — '

'At that point,' said Archer with

decision, 'we come clean. We pull the plug on ourselves, whatever the consequences.'

'I agree,' said Mitchell. 'And anyhow, what are the consequences? Macalister painted a pretty black picture, but wasn't he laying it on too thick? Should we have called his bluff? Told him to publish and be damned?'

'Wisdom after the event,' said Archer. 'But I'm quite satisfied we did the right thing. To lose the missile contract would have been bad enough in itself; but the knock-on effect would have been in my judgement total disaster. We've got to play things as they now are — and the first thing is to get to Macalister before the police do. In fact, with his half million waiting for my signature we should get a call from him any day now.'

14

Sergeant James Tough found himself walking up and down in front of the platinum and gold entrance to MIL House at five minutes past six, at slight risk to his professional career (for he had not told Inspector Robinson what he was up to) and perhaps at greater risk to his domestic bliss (for he had told his wife he was working late). The latter was strictly true but the work in question was anything but routine and it is possible that Mrs Tough, tolerant as she was, would have found it difficult to give it her wholehearted approval.

His sorties were carefully timed and a casual observer of only one of them would have deduced that he was walking smartly in the direction of the bus or underground that would take him back to the bosom of his loving family. The observer who concentrated on his total performance would have been mystified, for having proceeded some seventy-five yards beyond the MIL entrance in the direction of Cheapside, he then gave the appearance of a man having forgotten something — perhaps his umbrella or brief-case — turned on his heel and retraced his footsteps, this time proceeding seventy-five yards beyond MIL in the direction of St Paul's. However, his mystifying performance passed unnoticed in the stream of humanity pouring from the massive front doors of MIL House and sweeping to right and to left homeward bound.

Tough knew he was gambling, but it was a gamble worth taking, although it had already cost him twelve pounds of his own hard-earned money. It paid off on his fifth sweep. He had no difficulty in picking out the trim figure of Miss Penelope Warner as she came down the steps and it required only the smallest of manœuvres to station himself in her path, and indeed collide gently with her. He picked up her umbrella with an abject apology, and then expressed surprise.

'It's Miss Warner, isn't it? Sergeant

Tough. Maybe you don't remember?'

'Of course I do.'

They fell into step. Tough continued his apologetic outpourings.

'Sorry for being so clumsy. Hope there's no damage? Quite sure? Is your umbrella OK?'

Miss Warner assured him there was nothing to worry about. She asked what he was doing in the City at that hour.

'Barbican Centre,' he explained. '*Emperor Concerto* with Ashkenazy. Both favourites with me.' (That at least was true.) 'I don't suppose — '

'Suppose what?'

'You see, my wife is under the weather and has had to cry off. So I've got a ticket to spare. It's awful cheek, but if you happened to be free . . . ?'

'I've nothing on this evening,' said Miss Warner, 'but — '

'But you don't accept invitations from strange policemen?'

'It's not that. I'd love to come. I adore Beethoven and the London Symphony Orchestra, but — '

She seemed uncertain how to put it.

'You see, I really have an ulterior motive in accepting. I was thinking of getting in touch with you anyway, and meeting you like this seems, well, heaven-sent.'

Tough expressed surprise, not entirely because he had been equated with providence.

'There's something I want to tell you. Though of course I'm sure I'll enjoy the concert.'

'Good! That's settled! I'd planned to have coffee and sandwiches first. Suit you?'

It was not until the interval, after a moving performance of the *Emperor*, that the archivist unburdened herself.

'Can I speak freely? In confidence, I mean? It won't get back to MIL House?'

'Of course. This is entirely between us,' replied Tough mendaciously.

'I don't want to tell tales out of school — but I think there's something funny going on. I'm sure the papers you wanted to see weren't destroyed, not as part of the routine weeding. I keep a list of what's sent for pulping — part of my job

— and nobody ever suggested the USAL papers should go.

'They could have gone accidentally?'

'Possibly. The porters can be very careless and they don't know what's valuable and what's rubbish. But it's unlikely.'

Tough said:

'When we met you in the chairman's room the other day he seemed to think the papers *had* been destroyed.'

'The old dear doesn't know what he's talking about. It's true he has to sign the destruction lists from time to time but he never reads them and wouldn't understand them if he did.'

Miss Warner showed all the contempt of the low-paid professional for the highly paid amateur.

'I see,' said Tough. He went on:

'Macalister had access to the USAL papers?'

'Yes. That's what I wanted to tell you about. I know they were on the shelf three weeks ago. I was looking for something near them, and I'd have noticed a gap. Now, Mr Macalister was in several times in the following week. He has a desk in the store room where the papers are kept, so he can help himself to what he needs without troubling me.'

'Are the files bulky? I mean, could he easily have removed them? Without anybody seeing?'

'There are about thirty, but he could have taken them in his brief-case, three or four at a time. The more I think of it the more it seems he must have stolen them. And it may not be stealing — he may have needed them for his research.'

'Has he taken files away before?'

'Several times — but he's always told me.'

'But never a USAL file?'

'No. Now, why this interest in our files and Mr Macalister? If *I* can ask a question?'

This was difficult. Tough had intended the passage of information to be one way. What would Robinson say about unauthorized disclosures? He took a deep breath and burned his boats.

'You see — and this is in strict confidence, you understand?'

'Yes.'

'We think Macalister may also have removed papers from the PRO. Correspondence between USAL and the Government in World War II; and that he wanted to get hold of the USAL copies of the same correspondence. Why, we don't know. Unless you have any ideas?'

'Good heavens!' exclaimed Miss Warner. 'I've no idea why he wanted these papers, but obviously he would want *both* sets. So he *must* have taken ours.'

'Any idea where he is now? Did he ever mention going on holiday?'

'No. I really saw very little of him. He went straight to his desk, and got on with the job there. I hope you find him quickly. These papers were *my* responsibility and it won't do me any good if they have been stolen — by Macalister or anybody else.'

Back in the concert hall Tough found it difficult to concentrate on the final work in the programme — an interminable piece of cacophony by some composer he had never heard of. If Miss Warner was to be believed the culprit was Macalister; and Macalister could be found nowhere.

It seemed to add up. But that was not the only thing that took his mind off the music. Somehow Penelope Warner's hand had slipped into his and to his astonishment he had not found it necessary to disengage it.

Next day Sir Maurice Dyer had a brief interview with MIL's archivist, of which no record was made for the company's files.

'Well, my dear?' he said when she came into his room. 'What news?'

'You'll never believe it, Sir Maurice, but I didn't have to do a thing. Literally. He was actually lying in wait for me when I left the office last night. I ask you!'

'You mean *he* wanted to speak to *you*?'

'Pretended it was accidental, but I'd seen him from the top of the steps. Walking up and down. Very neatly done.'

'Well, I'm damned!' said the chairman. 'The bird does sometimes fly into the shot. Then what happened?'

'Took me to the Barbican — a jolly good concert. His wife was sick, so he had a spare ticket. Or so he said. I told him I was sure Mr Macalister has taken the

USAL files, like you said; and he told me, in confidence, that the police were sure he had taken papers from the PRO.'

'Well done!' said Dyer. 'I've no doubt this will help the course of justice. Putting the police on the right lines.'

'He *must* have taken our files, Sir Maurice. Will the company prosecute?'

'We'll have to wait and see what the police say — when they find him.'

★   ★   ★

Inspector Robinson was not sure whether to congratulate or reprimand his sergeant. He was annoyed that Tough should have taken it upon himself to interview Penelope Warner; but he could not deny that their *tête-à-tête* had probably been more profitable than a formal interview. At least he was now satisfied that first priority must be given to finding Macalister.

His Oxford college pointed out that it was the vacation and they were still sorry they couldn't help. He might be acquiring a tan in any one of the sun-providing

231

countries. No, he had left no forwarding address.

Robinson therefore arranged for his description to be circulated to police stations nationwide, in the hope that he was still in the country — and also that he had now dyed his crowning glory. He had not. Two days after the description went out a message was received from the Strathclyde police force relaying a report from Sergeant Tornadee in charge at the tiny seaport of Mallaig on the west coast of Scotland. Mr Macalister was holidaying quite openly in a chalet on the nearby estate. He came in from time to time to shop in Mallaig.

When Tough telephoned Tornadee to make sure he'd got the right Macalister, he became as rude as his highland nature would permit. He knew Mr Macalister of old. Yes, he was the one who wrote the history books. He had more than once spent a holiday on the local estate, and had not been averse to passing the time of day with the citizens of Mallaig, including Sergeant Tornadee.

What was he to do about him? The

answer was nothing more than to keep an unobtrusive eye on him until Sergeant Tough arrived — which he would do within the next twenty-four hours.

Before Tough set off on his highland journey he reminded Inspector Robinson of the coincidence that USAL, which was really MIL, papers had been stolen, and that the chairman of MIL had been kidnapped, which the inspector had written off as mere coincidence. Robinson reluctantly agreed that there might be more to it than met the eye, and that he would discuss with Scotland Yard. He even conceded that he might perhaps have got in touch with the Yard sooner.

He was received by Inspector Wainwright in his fourth-floor office in Victoria Street.

'The kidnapping stinks to high heaven,' said Wainwright, 'and we can't get through the smell. Maybe if we'd known earlier about the possible link with the Kew thing . . . At first the firm swore they were co-operating — passing on the ransom note and so on — and we had to believe them; but their co-operation was very selective. They showed us only what they wanted us to see, especially the note that led to that shambles at Wimbledon. A blind to put us off the scent while the real deal was going through somewhere else. They don't admit it but it sticks out a mile.'

'How was the money passed over?'

'We haven't a clue. Gilbert Archer, in charge while Dyer was missing, is a shrewd operator. Won't give a thing away. Kidnappers asked for half a million but we don't know what the firm settled for. I guess a lot less. Dyer is so vague about the whole thing it's unbelievable. True, he's an old man and pretty shook up, but for a chap who's supposed to be running one of the biggest companies in the world . . . They stopped his Rolls, blindfolded him and then drove him for hours on end. At least two men, who he says could be American from their accent. They were probably enterprising Cockneys. Taken to somewhere in Scotland which turned out to be Glencoe. Thinks he spent four days there, but lost all count of time — that's reasonable. Was fed on a diet of Spam and beer. Confirmed by the cans found in his hut. Only his fingerprints, which figures. How he survived four days there in that climate I simply don't know. I wouldn't. Then set free, presumably after the ransom was collected.'

'Or the kidnappers got cold feet?'

'If that had happened the firm would have told us.'

'What about the car they used? Automatic or manual? How many gears? Dyer must have heard the engine?'

'Says he's not much good at that sort of thing. Seems totally helpless. He may be just plain stupid, unlike Archer who's very much on the ball.'

'We might have another go at him,' suggested Robinson. 'Tell him we've now got our hands on Macalister — and that we think he stole their papers.'

'I'm not sure where we come in now,' said Wainwright. 'I mean on the kidnapping side.'

'Macalister had a hand in that as well?'

'Come off it,' replied Wainwright with a laugh. 'You can't pin everything on him. Theft from PRO, theft from MIL, kidnapping MIL's chairman.'

'And the murder of Kevin Wigmore,' said Robinson. 'Why, I don't yet know. But let's see what Jim Tough turns up in Scotland. Somebody killed Wigmore, and Macalister could have a better motive than most.'

15

The flight to Glasgow on the shuttle was without incident. Tough was politely received by a member of the Strathclyde Force and driven across the decaying wastes of Glasgow to the Queen's Hotel where he breakfasted off porridge, kippers, bacon and eggs, coffee, toast and marmalade before joining the quaint little train for Mallaig. After trundling, sometimes at little more than walking pace, for several hours through some of Scotland's most spectacular scenery, during which the only refreshment provided was a meat pie of dubious vintage and a can of McEwan's ale, the train deposited him at Mallaig, terminus of the West Highland Railway. He booked into the Sleat Hotel as plain Mr Tough before calling at the tiny police station to meet Sergeant Tornadee, whose alertness had brought him post-haste north of the border.

Tornadee, like most of his fellow countrymen, strongly deprecated accepting credit where none was due.

'It wass nothing at all,' he said gently. 'Mr Macalister has been coming here for his holidays two or three times before.' Tough found his Highland lilt, which it is impossible to convey in cold print, entirely engaging. 'A verra nice chentilman, we thought, for all his English speech and ways, though there are some of us who think he has a little bit of a swollen head. I think I would have recognized him from the description in your circular, even if I had not met him before. That hair of hiss, it iss unmistakable. Now, what hass he been up to, and what do you want me to do?'

Tough, anxious to get on with the job as quickly as possible, for there was little daylight left, gave a brief summary of the investigation into the Kew murder to which Tornadee listened attentively, without interruption. When he had finished Tough said:

'You say he's living in a chalet on an estate?'

'Yess. The MacGrail estate. I can show you where.'

Sergeant Tornadee rose and pointed to a large-scale Ordnance map of his territory hanging on the wall.

'The estate runs along the shores of Loch Nevis for about ten miles. The castle is at the far end — here — but the family have built six chalets which they let to visitors to help to make ends meet in these hard times. Mr Macalister has taken Lochnagar, the one nearest to the castle. They are all called after Scottish mountains, you see.'

'I could take the next-door chalet. I think I'd like to find out what he is doing — before he knows we're interested in him.'

'Yess, of course. At this time of year the chalets are usually all unoccupied. It came as a surprise when Mr Macalister arrived.'

'When did he arrive?'

'It would be — ' Sergeant Tornadee thought for a few moments — 'it would be about two weeks ago. We can get the date from the estate office here in

Mallaig. When you book yours. I'll take you there now.'

'Perhaps I'd better go on my own,' said Tough.

'That iss true,' agreed his colleague. 'It's at the end of the street. You can't miss it.'

The sole occupant of the office, on the glass door of which was inscribed 'MacGrail Estate', was a red-headed girl in her twenties. She was much surprised at getting a second out-of-season tenant, and enquired if Tough was a friend of Mr Macalister, also from London. He was a little disconcerted to find that the minimum booking was for a week, and he wondered how this would look on his expenses sheet. However, the formalities were safely completed and he found himself tenant of Benachie for seven days with the option to a further seven days if he found he could not tear himself away from the place.

Half an hour later he was cycling along the narrow road that ran through the MacGrail estate on the shore of Loch Nevis on a tall venerable machine with the square handlebars seldom seen on the road in this modern age. He had left his bags at the Sleat Hotel and had packed things for the night in a knapsack acquired at the town's general store. He was not quite sure what his plan of campaign should be but the first priority must be to visit to Macalister's chalet. It was quite possible the man was enjoying an innocent holiday; and if that was established the sooner he (Tough) made his way back to London the better.

He had been assured by the girl in the estate office that he would have reasonable privacy — each of the six chalets was surrounded by about four thousand acres, and they were spaced at two-mile intervals. Darkness was falling as he reached the track leading to Benachie, and he almost missed the discreet sign indicating the chalet. It was about three hundred yards down a side road, an attractive prefabricated Norwegian pine building with a good view of the loch and the mountains on the far shore, now almost invisible in the twilight.

Everything was as promised by the girl

in the estate office, including a pile of dry logs by the large brick fireplace, and a generous supply of firelighters. Within ten minutes Tough had a good fire going. Within another twenty he was sitting down to a meal of tinned soup, heated on the calor gas stove, and cold ham and tongue bought in Mallaig, the whole washed down by a couple of cans of beer, and topped up with the better part of a half bottle of Johnny Walker. The bed was harder than it need have been but after the exertions of the day the sergeant slept soundly enough.

Before he dropped off he briefly considered his plan of campaign for the morning. He *must* get within striking distance of Macalister's chalet without alerting the occupant, and have a general look round. Thereafter he would invite the historian to accompany him to London for questioning. If he refused to come, his instructions were to play it by ear, although he was not quite sure what that would mean.

He set his pocket alarm for seven-thirty but was awake long before that hour. The warmth from the huge fire he had built up to see him through the night had vanished. It was a cold and rather disgruntled sergeant that crawled out of bed and brewed himself a cup of tea. There seemed to be no means of making toast so he settled for two huge chunks of bread and butter. Thus fortified, he mounted his antediluvian bicycle and set off up the glen in the direction of Lochnagar, Macalister's chalet. As he approached it dawn was breaking and he wondered if he had left his expedition too late. He had hoped to reach the chalet before its tenant was up and about.

He estimated he had about half a mile to go when a steep rise slowed his progress. He had dismounted to take a breather when he heard ahead of him the sound of a car — somebody from the castle at the head of the glen, or perhaps his quarry. Whoever it was he must not be seen and he took the only possible avoiding action. He turned into the bracken at the side of the road, hoping it did not hide a fifty-foot precipice, and that he might find something reasonably soft to land on. He was in luck, for the bank down which he plunged sloped gently for about ten feet, terminating in a patch of peat bog, which provided a safe but smelly resting-place. He had time to collect himself and scramble up the bank before the approaching car came in sight.

It was Macalister's Jaguar, with the owner unmistakably at the wheel. No doubt heading to Mallaig to lay in provisions. This was a stroke of luck Tough had not bargained for.

With some difficulty he dragged the bicycle up the bank through the bracken and continued to pedal vigorously over the remaining half mile or so. There was a small sign indicating Lochnagar, and two minutes later Tough was outside the twin of his own chalet.

He had hoped that Macalister might have left it unlocked but was disappointed, and his own key failed to open either front or back door. He had to settle for peering through the windows and quickly came to the conclusion that Macalister must have left for good. Everything seemed to be tidied away

— pots, pans, crockery and the like. The bedding had been folded and the log fire was a heap of ashes. He had come on the scene an hour too late and cursed himself for not paying his visit the night before.

He was about to leave disconsolate, but first made a final tour of the chalet. There was a waste bin standing at the back door next to an incinerator — presumably in the absence of a local garbage collection tenants were required to burn their rubbish. Without much hope he looked in the bin, which contained nothing but old newspapers. Not very rewarding, he thought as he replaced the lid.

Then he removed it again and had a look at the papers. The *Sunday Times*, the *Sunday Telegraph*, the *Sunday Express*, and the *Observer* — all dated 16 January, the day Sir Maurice Dyer had been kidnapped. That was startling enough but what came as a real shock was the single word printed in pencil at the top right-hand corner of the front page of the *Observer*: Dyer.

Tough found it difficult to grasp the implications of this momentous discovery.

He remembered that Lady Dyer had suggested that the reason for her husband's early morning trip was to collect Sunday papers that had not been delivered. The newsagent had been quite certain that the papers had been delivered as usual, and here was evidence at least that they had left his shop destined for the Dyer residence.

How had the papers got to Macalister's chalet? And where did Macalister fit in? The sergeant found himself quite unable to arrive at rational explanations. Perhaps his superiors in London would have more success. The important thing was to get the news of his discovery to them without delay.

He carefully folded the papers and stowed them in his bicycle basket. He then made his way back to Benachie to pick up his haversack, and set off down the glen still trying in vain to find a logical connection between Dyer, Macalister and the newspapers.

After an hour's vigorous pedalling — downhill most of the way, for which he was thankful — he reached the town and made straight for the police station. Sergeant Tornadee was waiting for him in some agitation. He said:

'I wass about to come and look for you. I am afraid you haff lost him.'

Tough sat down thankfully, his legs aching from the use of forgotten muscles.

'You see,' went on Tornadee, 'he came here about an hour ago. Stopped at the garridge to fill up with petrol and then away he went. The garridge man thinks he iss on hiss way back to London at the end of hiss holiday. I would half detained him until you came back, Sergeant, but I haf no instructions.'

Tornadee seemed afraid that his inaction might have let the side down, and also that he had missed a possible moment of glory.

'That's all right. No harm,' replied Tough. 'I guessed as much. I nearly ran into him — or him into me. Just managed to get off the road in time. I couldn't get into his chalet — thought nobody ever locked a door in Scotland — but I hit the jackpot in the rubbish bin at the back. Don't know yet how much it's worth.'

He laid the newspapers on the sergeant's desk.

'I'd better call London right away.'

He was lucky enought to find Robinson in their room at the PRO. It took the inspector some time to believe the miracle.

'Get back here as quick as you can, Jim,' he said. 'I'll put this to Wainwright — and see where we go. It looks as if the Warner girl is right. Macalister *did* pinch the USAL files. And he must be tied up with the kidnapping as well. We'll have a reception committee waiting for him in Bloomsbury. With a warrant.'

'For murder?' asked Tough.

'Everything up to and including. See you.'

When Robinson put Wainwright in the picture about the discovery of the newspapers neither of them was able to guess how they had got to Macalister's chalet. The one point they were agreed on was that the historian had some explaining to do.

Wainwright rehearsed the various permutations and combinations suggested by the newspaper discovery.

Dyer had been kidnapped on the way back from the newsagent. But that wouldn't do since he had said he was stopped on the way to Esher. Moreover the young lady who served in the newsagent's had no doubt she would have remembered his visit. When his papers had not been delivered in the past (which had happened from time to time) he had made no secret of his views about the incompetent service; and there was no reason to think he would have reacted any differently on this occasion.

The newsagent himself had been adamant the papers *had* been delivered.

Could the kidnappers have collected them from Dyer's front door to while away the time waiting for him to emerge? This idea appealed to Wainwright. He said:

'It was well known in the newsagent's that Dyer went off at the deep end when he was denied his Sunday morning reading. So if you wanted to tempt him out of his lair, what better way than to remove his newspapers?'

'That argues local knowledge,' objected Robinson, 'and I don't see this as a local crime. And there's still Macalister to explain away.'

'How far is Glencoe from Macalister's chalet?'

'I think Jim Tough said about three hours' drive.'

'So the kidnap gang, having enticed Dyer out of the house by pinching his Sunday reading, drive him to Glencoe. Leave him there with say two men to guard him. The third — who must have been Macalister — drives on to the Mallaig chalet, taking the papers with him —'

'Why?'

'Perhaps he didn't realize they were in the car.'

'Have we got enough to go back to MIL?' asked Robinson.

'Good lord, yes. Aside from the newspapers, there's Miss Warner's certainty that Macalister took those files. Confidence or no confidence, MIL are entitled to know that one of their employees thinks another is a thief.'

'I suppose so,' agreed Robinson. 'And it does stick out that Macalister must have been on to something big — big enough for Wigmore to blackmail him, and big enough for him to kill Wigmore. OK. I'll make a date to see Sir Maurice Dyer.'

16

So far as the media were concerned the investigation of the murder at Kew had come to a disappointing full stop with the release of Julian Hardcastle; and the public at large, accustomed to follow the lead of the Press, radio and television, forgot Kew and settled for other dramas.

However, that small section of the community which availed itself of the facilities provided by the Public Record Office could not so easily forget the event that had put them all, at least momentarily, under a cloud of suspicion. As the days went by and the police seemed to be making no progress the regular readers at Kew became more and more vocal among themselves. When they deposited hats and coats in the morning, and collected lunches in the cafeteria they exchanged critical comments in loud voices so that all within earshot might be made aware of their dissatisfaction, and in some cases positive apprehension.

Miss Ernestine Dudley, who now regularly joined Richard Bodley for lunch, was typical of the record agents. She claimed that the police failure to make an arrest was beginning to interfere with her work.

'How can you concentrate,' she demanded, 'how can you *possibly* concentrate on a set of eighteenth-century Devonport dockyard accounts when you know that the person sitting next to you may be . . . '

She could not bring herself to say what that person might actually be.

Bodley was tempted to point out that for the last few weeks the person sitting next to her had been himself; but knowing she was genuinely upset by the possibility, perhaps even probability, that there was a murderer among the readers, he refrained. Although he knew he was himself innocent, he could not vouch for the person sitting on Miss Dudley's other side.

Sometimes he sought relaxation after a long session poring over his records by strolling round the Reading Room. Then he found himself studying his fellow readers and wondering how many of them would be capable of murder. Worse, which of them had disposed of Kevin Wigmore.

Perhaps it was the fellow feeling induced by the strained atmosphere that brought about a half rapprochement with Michael Carrington. One day the only vacant place in the cafeteria was at the table shared by Bodley and Miss Dudley. Carrington, with laden tray, looked in vain elsewhere, and Bodley could hardly refrain from motioning him to join them.

After an awkward five minutes in which the pair enquired about their progress in their respective research fields, the conversation inevitably came round to the murder. Carrington strove to allay Ernestine Dudley's fears by saying he had no doubt the murderer was a bird of passage.

'I don't know what the attendance figures are,' he went on, 'but I guess the number of regular readers like us is small. Most people finish their work in a few days, and then never come back. In any case, the murderer would be crazy to come back and risk giving himself away. No, Miss Dudley, you can sleep happily in your seat. Take my word for it.'

'You're not just saying that, Mr Carrington?'

'I mean every word. Forget that it ever happened.'

'That's just what I can't do,' replied Miss Dudley with a shudder. 'When I think of that day — '

'Don't,' said Bodley. 'Put it out of your head.'

'That's easier said than done.'

This was true. Any individual effort to put the murder out of mind was frustrated by the regular presence of Peter Plumb's BBC TV crew. Television cameras were a common enough sight in the PRO. Teams from the BBC and ITV and the American and Japanese networks were constantly visiting the Reading Room to photograph records to illustrate documentary programmes; but these were friendly projects, welcome because they often provided employment for the record agents. Peter Plumb's team, on the other hand were seen as a sinister, if not actually ghoulish, group. There was a general feeling that wherever their camera pointed, there pointed the finger of suspicion.

★ ★ ★

When Sir Maurice Dyer heard that Inspector Robinson and Inspector Wainwright wanted to see him again he was filled with alarm. The two investigations in which MIL was more or less directly involved — the theft of the wartime memorandum from the PRO and the kidnapping of their chairman — had come together. The police must be getting near to the truth. If there was to be a final showdown Dyer felt he must have the support of the other members of his inner cabinet. So when the two inspectors were shown into the chairman's office they found themselves facing the three senior directors.

'There are some things we don't understand,' explained Wainwright when they had shaken hands. 'We hope you can help us. Mainly about the kidnapping, on which we have some news for you.'

'Well done!' said Dyer, with an enthusiasm he certainly did not feel.

Robinson took up the tale.

'We've at last tracked down the elusive Macalister,' he said. 'We circulated his description and had a reply from Mallaig in Scotland saying he was holidaying there. In a chalet a few miles from the town.'

'Funny time of year for a Scottish holiday,' observed Gilbert Archer.

'No accounting for tastes, sir,' agreed Robinson.

'At least it's all above board,' said Bernard Mitchell.

'We sent Sergeant Tough up there,' went on Robinson. 'He's working with us, you know. To interview Macalister about the memorandum missing from the PRO, but he just missed him. Tough had a look round the chalet, and found *these*.'

He pulled the four newspapers from his briefcase and spread them before the chairman.

'Your Sunday papers, sir. Which were

never delivered that day.'

'God bless my soul,' cried Dyer. 'What an extraordinary thing! How on earth did they find their way to Scotland?'

'The kidnappers must have taken them while they were lying in wait for you. Then when you saw there were no papers, and went off to collect them, you made their job a bit easier. In fact, they may even have known that you were in the habit of going to Esher when the newsagent left you off his round. Unless you have a better idea?'

The three directors exchanged glances. Dyer shook his head.

'What does come out clearly,' said Wainwright, 'is that Mr Macalister is in this right up to his neck. Inspector Robinson suspects he's responsible for the theft *and* murder in the PRO — this is in confidence, he hasn't been charged. And these newspapers must mean he was involved in your kidnapping.'

'This is unbelievable,' said Dyer. 'Quite unbelievable. But if you're satisfied . . . ?'

'It would strengthen our case,' said Robinson, 'if you were able to tell us something more about your kidnappers. Can you be quite sure that Macalister wasn't one of them?'

Dyer frowned and said:

'It all happened so quickly.'

'If you could run over the events for us again, sir?'

Dyer now thought furiously, trying to remember exactly what he had told the police last time round. He even wondered whether the inspector was trying to lead him into a trap to get a conflicting statement which might give the game away.

'There were two men, I think you said,' prompted Wainwright.

'I saw only two. Both wearing masks.'

'Neither of them was Macalister?'

'Of course not. I'd have recognized him. His hair, and voice, would be unmistakable. And if he had been there I would certainly have told you when I last made a statement.'

'Of course,' said Wainwright soothingly. 'Could there have been a third man? Who kept out of sight until you were blindfolded?'

'It's possible. If Macalister was there he wouldn't have wanted to come face to face with me. But he could have joined the party later. *En route*, or at Glencoe. Though I don't remember stopping to pick anybody up.'

'When they finally left you,' said Wainwright, 'you didn't see the car, or get its number?'

'My hands were still tied,' said Dyer, 'and I was blindfolded. By the time I had freed myself they were a long way down the hill. All I saw was its lights disappearing.'

'I see,' said Wainwright. He sounded disappointed. 'Well, I think that's about all. Unless Inspector Robinson has any further questions?'

'No,' said Robinson. 'We had hoped that in the light of this new information — about the missing newspapers — we might get a bit nearer the truth. The evidence against Macalister is to my mind conclusive — as to the kidnapping, I mean; but I don't think the case would stand up in court. However, we've got enough to go on without it.'

'You have?' said Gilbert Archer.

'Yes. The case against him for the theft of the PRO papers is cut and dried. We found the memorandum in his bed-sitter this morning. That's enough to pin the murder on him too.'

'But not the kidnapping,' said Wainwright. 'So we don't get our hat trick. Unless there is something else you can tell us? For example, who did you pay the ransom to, and how was it paid?'

'I'm sorry, Inspector,' said Archer quickly before his colleagues could speak. 'I know how you feel about that. Put our refusal down to a question of commercial judgement, and not to any wish to hinder the police. We're most grateful for your efforts.'

As the two policemen rose to go the telephone on the chairman's desk rang.

'It's for you, Inspector Robinson,' he said.

Robinson took the instrument and listened for a moment.

'Good show,' he said. 'That was Sergeant Tough,' he explained as he hung up. 'Macalister is now under arrest. For the theft of a public document. For the murder of Kevin Wigmore.'

'But not for alleged kidnapping,' said Archer.

'Like I said,' said Wainwright. 'Insufficient evidence and if you'll forgive me, gentlemen, insufficient cooperation. You *might* have had a chance of seeing your half million again. As it is . . . '

He left the sentence unfinished and the two policemen left the room. Sir Maurice Dyer locked the door behind them and made a beeline for the cocktail cabinet in the corner of his office. He poured three generous Scotches and made a toast.

'To the Devil,' he said. 'Who looks after his own.'

'I'm not sure that I can drink to that, Maurice,' said Mitchell who had had a puritanical upbringing.

'Whoever it is,' observed Archer, drinking deeply, 'we are indebted to *someone*. What happens now?'

'Think it through,' said Dyer. 'And thank your lucky stars. Macalister is charged with theft and murder. He is not to be charged with kidnapping, I suspect because the police are irritated by our non-co-operation, and want to punish us. And we are delighted to be thus punished.'

'But what about Macalister?' asked Bernard Mitchell. 'What's he going to say about all this?'

'That's the beautiful part of it,' said Archer. 'Even if he's convicted of both the theft and the murder, he says nothing — unless he wants to cut off our nose to spite his face. If he's convicted, and he may not be, he serves his sentence, and collects half a million at the end of it. If he spills the beans, he gets nothing.'

'We set up a sort of murderer's trust?' asked Mitchell. 'To realize half a million plus interest in twenty years time? When I doubt if any of us will be around to administer the trust.'

'There's no guarantee he will be convicted,' said Dyer. 'All we can do for the moment is to sit tight and await developments. And get permission for one of us to have a discreet word with him before the trial comes off.'

17

Inspector Robinson, who in the earlier days of the investigation had been reluctant to perform before the camera, now seemed confident enough to face it with something approaching enthusiasm. He had invited Ernest Pepperbred to be present to deal with any technical administrative questions that might crop up. Others who were not averse to contributing to the performance were the keeper, who in any case was required to hold a watching brief because of his responsibility for the institution, and his two deputies. Sergeant Tough was there to support the inspector. Peter Plumb and his film crew were supplemented for the occasion by Jeremy Whitaker whom Peter wanted to join in what might be the last filming session. After all, had it not been for Jeremy's support his documentary would never have got off the ground.

Robinson was seated at a table flanked

by the keeper and the sergeant. As the camera began to roll he had a mild attack of stage fright, but soon recovered and got into his stride.

'To begin at the beginning, we're dealing with four crimes, separate, but related. Theft of a public document, consequential blackmail and murder, and kidnapping. As you know, our first real clue to the theft was the erased entry in the surveillance record, spotted by Sergeant Tough. Pretty smart, and took a sharper eye than mine. That led us to believe that whoever was sitting at Table 8 H during lunch that day had stolen a World War II memorandum. No reader's name was recorded in the surveillance record, as offenders are in the first instance identified only by their table number.

'On the face of it then, it looked as if Wigmore had spotted a serious offence and changed his mind about reporting it. Why? We turned up a motive in double quick time. The Wigmores, happily married, want to move up market. Mrs Wigmore's two thousand pounds with the building society make it possible. Then dry rot hits them for six. I've had it — nothing as bad as theirs — and I can tell you it's a killer. So Wigmore now needs a bundle of money. Takes five hundred from the building society without telling his wife, hies himself to Kempton Park to find a couple of winners at ten to one, so easy, don't we all know. Blues the lot. Three race meetings later the whole two thousand is gone, together with Wigmore's up-market ambitions, and any hope of coping with their dry rot problem. What now? He's really desperate — when 8 H comes to his rescue.

'Now, who was at 8 H? The computer told us Julian Hardcastle. The memorandum was stolen from a file requisitioned on *his* reader's number. That seemed conclusive. When we interrogated him his actions confirmed that he was guilty. But it turned out that this was simply an act try to increase the sales of his books. With what success I don't know.'

'I believe his sales have doubled,' observed the keeper.

'Up to two dozen a year,' added one of his deputies *sotto voce*.

'There's no doubt in my mind,' continued Robinson, 'that he was deliberately hindering the police in the execution of their duty, and should be made to answer for it. But we decided to let the matter drop. We had bigger fish to fry. We now accept that somebody else must have used Hardcastle's reader card and table number to saddle him with the removal of the memorandum.'

'You can't *positively* rule out Hardcastle,' suggested the keeper. 'You've only his word for it he didn't take the memorandum — and he *was* there on the day, you know. *And* on the day of the murder.'

'He'd no motive, as far as we can discover. The file the memorandum was removed from was odd man out. Nothing to do with his subject. The computer could be used to play a trick like that. You said so yourself, Keeper.'

The inspector seemed aggrieved.

'It doesn't follow it *was* a trick,' said the keeper.

'Leave Hardcastle on one side,' said the inspector irritably. 'Think of the others who stayed late on the Wednesday of the murder. Luckily not many, and most of them elderly women record agents and schoolchildren who couldn't use a heavy paperweight — at least not *that* way. Of the possibles — which we took to mean people who were present the day Hardcastle was set up — ' he went on in spite of a muttered grumble from the unrepentant keeper — 'and stayed late on Wednesday — there was Mr Bodley.

'Now, he had begun to work in the PRO in rather peculiar circumstances. After his furniture was stolen when it was not covered by insurance. He was forced to take a job as research assistant to his friend Carrington; but it lasted only a week or two before Carrington told him his services were no longer required. Why, we don't really know. Carrington said he couldn't afford an assistant — but surely he must have known that when he took Bodley on.'

'Maybe Bodley was just plain incompetent,' suggested one of the deputy keepers. 'And Carrington was too polite to tell him.'

'Be that as it may, Mr Bodley, helped by friends he made in the PRO, decided to become a record agent in his own right, to offer research services to anyone who wanted to hire him. To help to make ends meet, after his financial disaster.'

'Bodley was more likely to have it in for Carrington, who had let him down, than for Hardcastle,' said the keeper. 'As he was broke, he could have had an incentive for blackmail.'

The inspector felt that he was being upstaged and that things were not going to plan. He went on quickly:

'We thought of all that. Bodley could certainly have done with some ready cash, but there was no sign that he had a hold over anybody. It's true big fleas have little fleas in blackmail as in other activities. If you *know* somebody is a blackmailer, he's ready-made for *your* blackmail. Bodley could have been trying to get a piece of Wigmore's action.'

To his eternal discredit, Inspector Robinson occasionally watched American

TV crime series, and even identified himself with the heroes therein. He continued:

'On the other hand, Bodley isn't the type. A law-abiding citizen all his career. A bit of a stick-in-the-mud who even had to be bullied by an old lady into trying his hand at a job here where your overheads and raw materials are provided free by a benevolent state, and your only outlay is on a pencil and paper. I'm not one of your psychological investigators, thank God, but Bodley is out on psychological grounds. He couldn't bring himself to steal a half new p.'

'Who does that leave?' asked the keeper.

'Somebody who provided Wigmore with a golden opportunity.'

The inspector interrupted his recital with a belly-laugh that caught Peter Plumb's sound recordist by surprise.

'Golden opportunity!' he repeated. 'That's rich! Very rich indeed! The computer told us Hardcastle was sitting at 8 H but Wigmore using the eyes God gave him, and none of your newfangled electronics, knew the truth. Hardcastle is bald, like not a few other readers. Too much thinking is bad for the hair. Macalister is a one-off. His golden curls are unmistakable even on a small black and white monitor screen. So the dry rot makes Wigmore a blackmailer and his golden curls make Macalister a murderer.'

'I'm not so sure,' put in the keeper. 'Don't know I'd give you my vote if I were on your jury.'

'There's more,' replied the inspector.

He paused to pour a glass of water from the carafe that Pepperbred had earlier placed before him.

'We now come to the most extraordinary part of the story. As you know, the chairman of MIL was kidnapped and then released unharmed. That can mean only one thing. The company paid the ransom. They've refused to give us any details — as they're quite entitled to do, though you may think them stupid; but we now have reason to believe that their own historian Macalister was one of the kidnap gang.'

'How?' demanded the keeper.

'Sir Maurice Dyer's Sunday newspapers, which he thought had not been delivered on the day of the kidnapping turned up in a hide-out hired by Macalister. Near Mallaig, not very far from the hut in Glencoe where Dyer was held. Dyer can't identify Macalister as one of the men who abducted him, but then he was blindfolded most of the time, and no doubt Macalister would have kept well in the background.

'Now Macalister was already on our short list of suspects. He was in the PRO at the time Hardcastle was framed. He was there on the Wednesday of the murder. To make assurance doubly sure he tried to pin the theft of the memorandum on somebody else. By choosing Hardcastle he made a silly mistake.'

'A fatal mistake,' put in the keeper. 'By picking on Hardcastle he drew attention to himself — because of the row they'd had — which was quite unnecessary.'

'That is so.'

Robinson seemed none too pleased by

this interruption. He went on:'

'All criminals make a mistake, sooner or later. If they didn't — '

'You'd never catch any,' suggested the more talkative deputy keeper.

The inspector pointedly ignored this contribution and went on:

'Correspondence is a two-way affair. Like trade. When I write to you I keep a copy, if I'm a business firm, that is; and so do you when you write to me. Our files are sort of mirror images of each other. But when we asked MIL to allow us to study *their* mirror image of the file from which the memorandum had been stolen, we were told it couldn't be found. The whole series of files, those of United Special Alloys Limited, had disappeared.'

'All of them?' asked the keeper.

'Yes.'

'That's odd. I should have expected them to preserve at least one or two. For sentimental reasons, if for nothing else. but paper does accumulate, and has to be disposed of. A matter of regret.'

'However,' resumed the inspector, 'thanks to the initiative and enterprise of

Sergeant James Tough here, who may have gone further beyond the line of duty than was strictly necessary — we won't enquire too deeply into that — we came to the conclusion that Macalister had stolen the USAL files also.'

'Just what did Sergeant Tough do?' asked Peter Plumb from the back of the room, anxious to bring a new face into his documentary.

'I'm coming to that,' replied the inspector, a little worried lest his subordinate steal the show. 'When Sergeant Tough first called on the MIL archivist she couldn't lay hands on the USAL papers, and had no idea what had happened to them. It was possible they'd been destroyed, like the keeper said just now. As part of a routine weeding-out exercise. But Tough thought there was more to it than met the eye . . . '

He paused to allow the sergeant to say his piece.

'I took her out for the evening. She said when I first saw her she hadn't wanted to accuse a colleague, but now she wanted me to know the truth — off the record.

She had no doubt that Macalister had stolen the files. *Why*, she couldn't tell.'

'So everything pointed to him,' resumed Robinson.

'Still nothing conclusive,' murmured the keeper, who seemed to have appointed himself Robinson's evil genius. The inspector braced himself for the *coup de grâce*.

'We were watching Macalister's bed-sitter in Bloomsbury. When he got back from Scotland we called on him with a warrant for the theft of a public document, and for the murder of Kevin Wigmore.'

'Not for the kidnapping?' asked the keeper.

'We don't need the kidnapping,' replied the inspector. 'We're settling for the murder. He was a bit slow in answering our knock, and when we did get in there was a smell of burning. He'd tried to get rid of the stolen memorandum, but his little gas fire hadn't done the trick. The body of the thing had gone up in smoke, but the corners of some of the pages — folios — remained. The numbers corresponded to the missing folios, and that was enough to cook his goose. We'll never know what was in the memorandum. But that's now a matter of academic interest.'

'How was it done?' asked the keeper. 'The murder, I mean? And has he admitted it?'

'He admitted the theft,' replied Robinson. 'He could hardly deny it. But not the murder. He'll come round in time. Must have gone into the stackroom to have a showdown with Wigmore. Lost his temper, or maybe did him in deliberately. Don't matter. Point is it was done, and only Macalister could have done it.'

'It was done all right!'

Peter Plumb's voice came dramatically from the end of the room where the camera was still turning.

'But not by Macalister. He *couldn't* have done it. It could have happened the way you say; but I'm afraid it didn't. Macalister never went into the stackroom that Wednesday afternoon.'

18

'I agree it could have happened as the inspector suggests,' repeated Peter. 'Or almost. But it didn't.'

The assembled company turned towards him in astonishment, except his camera crew, whom he had warned to hold themselves in readiness for a dramatic climax to their documentary. A new magazine was loaded in the camera and two replacements were made ready — enough film to take care of all eventualities. The crew were more than ever convinced that the BAFTA documentary of the year award was theirs for the taking.

Jeremy Whitaker was less confident. Indeed he was beginning to wonder if he had been wise in accepting Peter Plumb's invitation to attend the session. If the young man was going to make a fool of himself and the institution he represented, he (Jeremy) would be better off polluting the atmosphere in his comfortable fourth-floor lair in Kensington House. On the other hand if against all the odds Peter was going to pull off a great coup . . .

'Of course, Inspector, there is a strong case against Macalister. For the murder. There's no argument about the theft of the memorandum. As you know, he was my tutor at Oxford and after a few terms you get to know your tutor even better than he knows you. A sad thought but there it is. So I can see him as a thief. A scholar who puts cash above scholarship can easily turn to a lazier way of making his pile, if the opportunity arises. But I can't see him as a murderer. That calls for the sort of nerve he simply hasn't got.'

'Every murderer isn't seen as a murderer by someone,' grumbled the inspector. 'If it's only his mother.'

'I'm not even his father, thank goodness,' said Peter.

'If it wasn't Macalister,' said Robinson, 'who's your substitute? Or don't you have one?'

'I've got one all right,' replied Peter

confidently. 'Let's go back to square one.'

He paused to cast a surreptitious glance at his team tucked away at the far end of the room to satisfy himself they had everything under control.

'It's now accepted that Wigmore was killed round about five o'clock on 29th December. Thanks to a complicated investigation by the police alibis have been provided for all his colleagues. So he must have been killed by a reader. The only readers in the field are those who were still working in the Reading Room after four o'clock on that Wednesday afternoon.'

'Ancient history,' muttered Robinson under his breath.

Plumb went on unabashed:

'The estimated time of death is important. 'About five o'clock' would be good enough for most murder investigations, but not in the present case. Since the Reading Room closes at five, it means that if the murder happened at say ten to five, it could have been done by a reader. If it was at ten past five, when the readers had all gone, it would seem that a member of the staff did it — in spite of their all-embracing alibi.'

'Nonsense!' said the keeper. 'I've seen Inspector Robinson's report. It's quite conclusive.'

'I agree,' said Peter, 'but the fact remains that if the murder had happened *after* five, Macalister can't be guilty. The computer shows he left *before* five. Now, let me remind you which readers were in the field. First, Julian Hardcastle, who allowed himself to be suspected for his own purposes, but is now in the clear, if only because Macalister tried to incriminate him. Which the keeper said just now was a fatal mistake. That's true, but only with the benefit of hindsight.'

'How d'ye mean?' asked the keeper.

'Think. Macalister must have known there was an outside chance the surveillance would spot him tampering with a file. When, against all the odds he *is* spotted, he is given a second chance by Wigmore's attempt to blackmail him; and but for the murder that second chance would have come off. Macalister would have paid off Wigmore, Wigmore would have moved house to Wimbledon, and at some remote date in the future somebody would have spotted that twenty folios were missing from that file, without having any idea why. So you see it wasn't really a fatal mistake of Macalister's making. It was the murder that got in the way, and the full-scale police investigation that followed. If Macalister had had any inkling about that, he would never have tried to play a trick on Hardcastle. I believe all this helps to clear him of the murder.'

'The other late Wednesday readers,' said Jeremy Whitaker. 'Which of them have you elected?'

'The schoolboys and the lady record agents rule themselves out, we're agreed. The only other is Richard Bodley, whose arrival in the PRO was strange, to say the least of it. A retired lawyer, leading a blameless life in his village, is suddenly introduced to the business of research by his friend Michael Carrington, after he has suffered a severe financial blow when the entire contents of his house are removed when they're not insured. For a short time Bodley is the paid assistant of his friend, and his financial worries are ended. Then suddenly his employment stops, and he's on his beam-ends again. He has a grudge against life in general and his former friend in particular. If anybody has an incentive for blackmail it's Richard Bodley. He also has a motive against Carrington.'

'Don't see how any of this fits,' said Robinson. 'We looked at the row between Bodley and Carrington. It was purely domestic, between themselves, and couldn't have anything to do with the murder.'

'Yes and no,' replied Peter Plumb.

Robinson seemed suddenly to realize the implications of the line Peter was taking.

'Hold on a minute,' he said angrily. 'I'm damned if I'm going to be made a fool of in front of your camera. When we agreed you should follow this investigation it was understood it would be *our* investigation. If you know something we don't it's your duty to pass it on, and not suppress it in the interests of your bloody film. You're an ordinary member of the public and you've no right to withhold information. It's our responsibility — '

'Of course it's your responsibility, and your investigation,' agreed Peter, unruffled. 'And I *am* passing on ideas for you to act on as you see fit.'

Robinson seemed to be unconvinced. He asked:

'What happens to your last bit of film? The case against Macalister — which you say doesn't stand up?'

Jeremy Whitaker thought it time to intervene.

'Inspector,' he said, 'surely the first priority is to bring the murderer to book? I don't know what Peter has up his sleeve, but this is the first chance he's had of putting it to you. It may be a funny way of doing it, but this whole business is something out of the ordinary.'

'You can say that again,' said the inspector.

He glowered, feeling he was being pushed into a corner. With difficulty he refrained from saying anything more, suspecting it might be used in evidence against him by several million viewers.

Whitaker said:

'After all, you had a fair crack of the whip just now, setting out the case against Macalister, proving him a thief. It will make darned good television, even if he isn't the murderer.'

That was true, thought the inspector. He sat back and waited, vowing not to utter another word. Tough, not bound by his superior's vow of silence, ventured to ask:

'Who *is* your replacement for Macalister?'

Plumb paused before dropping his bombshell. Then he said:

'Any one of the two hundred readers in the PRO on that Wednesday — except those who were still there after four o'clock.'

He paused again to let this sink in.

'Good God, man!' cried the inspector, forgetting his vow. 'You must be mad! You've got the whole thing upside down. We all agreed the only possible suspects were people there late on Wednesday.'

'We did,' said Peter calmly. 'And we

were all wrong. We fell headfirst into the pit dug for us by the murderer. It was only last night I saw the light; and as Jeremy says this is the first chance I've had to put you in the picture.'

Robinson lapsed into silence again. He wondered how his claim that Macalister was the murderer would come out on the screen. The scholar might even have a libel or slander case against him. Peter Plumb went on:

'When we were going back to the office after filming yesterday — me and my crew — we took the Underground at Piccadilly Circus. Jackie — our assistant cameraman — bought the tickets and fed all six into the turnstile as the rest went through. But before he followed us through he remembered he'd left his gear by the ticket machine. When he got back to the turnstile he'd lost his place in the queue, and had therefore also lost his ticket.'

'I don't see — ' said Robinson.

'I do,' murmured his sergeant. 'Christ Almighty!'

Peter went on:

'So far as the turnstile was concerned all six of us, including Jackie, had gone through. *Now* do you see? The same thing can happen in the PRO — with the difference that the traffic there moves in both directions, in *and* out. Unlike the Underground where you don't leave through a turnstile.'

'That's it!' said Tough, well up with the ball. His superior, who was not, gave him an angry look.

Plumb resumed his exposition:

'If I want to remain overnight in the PRO and to have a perfect alibi, what do I do? I give my reader's card to a friend. He leaves at say two o'clock, feeds his own card into the exit turnstile, goes through, leans over to feed in the other card, moves the turnstile barrier one notch forward, retrieves his friend's card, and hey presto! the computer records that both readers have left.'

'Taking a bit of a risk,' suggested the keeper, who had been following the argument intently. 'Wouldn't the security guards spot the manœuvre?'

'Not if I choose the psychological

moment. There's a steady stream of readers in the early forenoon and later afternoon, when you'd stand a good chance of being seen by another reader and by the security guards; but there's little movement in the forenoon and the middle of the afternoon. In any case, if I think I'm going to be spotted, I pause to admire a picture, or at worst go back upstairs to pretend to look up a reference. I carry out my double exit act only when I'm certain the coast is clear.'

'And next day you reverse the process?' said the keeper.

'Exactly. Same thing t'other way round. My accomplice, again choosing a dead period, posts in both reader cards. Now both of us are back inside the magic circle, no questions asked.'

'But one of you has to get into and out of the stackroom without being seen?'

'That's right, Keeper. A more difficult problem. He slips in after the paternoster staff have gone home at four, and while Wigmore is at tea.'

'Still risky,' observed the keeper. 'He

could walk into some other member of the staff.'

'Of course. Then he says he was looking for the loo, or something of the sort. Apologizes for his silly mistake. Ten times out of ten that would be accepted and the matter forgotten.'

'Not if there had been a murder.'

'No-one knew there had been a murder. No-one intended there should be a murder. It was a spur of the moment job — which made the consequences of being seen coming out of the stackroom much more serious. But he had to take the risk; and he got away with it.'

'If we accept all this,' said Inspector Robinson, not yet convinced that his case against Macalister was dead and buried, 'we're left with two hundred suspects. Every single person in the Reading Room could have used the turnstile gadgetry to give themselves an alibi?'

'Not every *single* person,' corrected Peter Plumb. 'Every *double* person, if you see what I mean. I spent this morning looking at the computer print-outs — to discover if a pair of readers left within a few seconds of each other on Wednesday afternoon.'

'With the same pair arriving next morning?'

'Yes. Now, there was a difficulty. In the ordinary course there must always be several 'natural' pairs. A husband and wife working together could well enter and leave at the same time, or say a father wanting to show his son a file dealing with a wartime operation he was on, or two people collaborating on a book. I found several pairs like this and rejected them. This left two pairs, both of which left in the 'dead' period of Wednesday afternoon, and returned at the end of the busy period on Thursday morning. It seemed to be a toss-up between them.'

'How did you choose, Peter?' asked Jeremy Whitaker, now satisfied his colleague was on to a winner.

'We could have confronted the two pairs and I dare say the truth would have emerged. Instead, I put myself into the mind, or rather the shoes, of the murderer. I followed him step by step through Wednesday to Thursday when the body was discovered. What do I do? I arrive in the morning, check in my coat as I am required to do by the regulations. (I might use it to smuggle out documents.) I then post my reader card through the turnstile and my presence is duly recorded by the computer.

'I spend the rest of the day carrying out my research, at some point hand my reader card to my accomplice, then wait my chance to slip into the stackroom when nobody is looking. If I am seen, I play the loo card. However, I get in all right, spend an uncomfortable night achieving my objective, and then next day make my getaway. Now, you see the fatal flaw?'

All faces were blank. Then the keeper, familiar with the regulations, said:

'Your coat?'

'Full marks,' said Peter approvingly. 'If the cloakroom attendant sees a left-behind coat at the end of the day there's the devil of a fuss. Somebody must still be in the building, and there will be hell to pay if they're not found.'

'A reader might simply have forgotten

his coat,' suggested Sergeant Tough.

'The staff still have to make certain no-one has stayed behind. In any case, in the depths of winter no-one in his senses will walk from this pleasantly warm building into sub-zero temperatures without noticing he's forgotten his coat. So my coat left in the cloakroom is a fatal error.'

'How d'ye get round it?' asked Robinson, interested in spite of himself. 'Wait for summer?'

'I don't check in a coat.'

'Your accomplice could collect it,' said the keeper.

'Too risky. My ploy depends on there being no connection between me and him.

Robinson, who had been slowly digesting Plumb's statement, now spluttered with excitement and cried, totally oblivious of the camera:

'This makes the case against Macalister! You told me yourself he was a fresh-air fiend — that he used to jog round the Parks half-naked even in mid-winter!'

Peter Plumb looked pityingly at Robinson.

'That was a piece of bad luck for you, Inspector. His masochistic habits did make him a possible suspect; but the mere fact that he was in the Reading Room on Wednesday afternoon lets him out. In any case, I had a ready-made substitute.'

'Who is?'

'Michael Carrington.'

Robinson, who by now ought to have know better, gave a cry of triumph.

'This time I *know* you've got it wrong! I can tell you — not for the record — that Carrington is a former member of M.I.6.'

Peter Plumb looked positively embarrassed, rather as a Wimbledon champion might look when pitted against an elderly vicar at a country house party. Because of his embarrassment he plunged deeper into the mire:

'Quite! I'll refrain from mentioning the incidence of the unsound produce of the *Pyrus Malus* tree in a cylindrical wooden vessel — '

'Peter!' cried Jeremy Whitaker, horrified.

'I think he means,' said the keeper, 'there's always one rotten apple in the barrel.'

'I'm sorry,' said Peter contritely. 'M.I.6 or 66 or 666, is not a guarantee of soundness. In the light of recent history Carrington's form of rottenness may be better than some.'

Robinson now appeared to be completely deflated. Peter went on:

'Carrington was one of a pair that 'left' on Wednesday afternoon. He was immediately preceded by Professor Thrasher. On Thursday forenoon the pair 'returned' — Thrasher immediately followed by Carrington. That made them possible suspects. What clinched it was Carrington's sartorial performance. When he started here in the autumn he came in coatless and hatless. Made sense then but he never wore a coat even on the foulest winter day. The front door attendant used to pull his leg about it. So on that freezing Wednesday his appearance caused no surprise. He probably had a double ration of long johns.'

Peter paused to observe how his audience was reacting. He went on:

'This made it clear that Carrington had been planning whatever he was up to for several months. It also implied Wigmore's murder was unpremeditated. He caught Carrington in the act, and got knocked on the head.

'Where does Bodley come in?' asked Tough.

'Carrington had to have an accomplice — somebody he could trust implicitly. At first Bodley was the best he could find and when Bodley refused to help he engineered the removal of his household goods. I guess — and it's only a guess — that Carrington in his M.I.6 days moved in shady places and was able to whistle up the fake furniture removers when he heard that Bodley's insurance had lapsed.

'Then — before he had told Bodley what was really required of him, he came across Professor Thrasher, who turned out to be a much better bet for his purposes than the timid Bodley. So he made his friend redundant and teamed up with Thrasher.'

'Thrasher was rushing off to the airport when we arrived that day,' remarked Tough, who had been running over the earlier evidence in his mind. 'And Rollem told us Thrasher had consulted him about something which meant leaving the Reading Room and going into the Reference Room.

'One pair of eyes less to contend with,' agreed Peter.

'All very interesting,' observed the keeper. 'Opportunity, yes. Motive? If he wasn't being blackmailed by Wigmore, why was he in the stackroom at all? What *was* his objective?'

'I can make a good guess,' replied Peter. 'After our coffee break. Equity rules, you know.'

19

After the coffee break, during which the keeper departed to his own office, the atmosphere became more relaxed. Inspector Robinson seemed to accept that Peter Plumb had something to contribute. He tried to visualize the end product — not the trial and conviction of Wigmore's killer, but rather the TV documentary and in particular his own role in it. It did not need a degree in psychology to grasp that he would make a better showing if he did not try to prove Peter Plumb wrong at every turn, if in fact the young man was right.

'What I've been saying so far,' resumed Peter, when all were in their places again, except the keeper, who had not yet returned, 'is supported by the facts.'

'Agreed,' said Inspector Robinson, anxious to get his new attitude on the record.

'What I'm now going to say is

speculation. First, Carrington's objective was to steal official papers, not just a single document, like Macalister, but on the grand scale. Few records are worth much in the open market — I mean modern records, you could retire on the proceeds of a black market sale of Magna Carta — but there are exceptions. The thing Macalister stole must have had some value, why I can't think. Some groups still closed to the public could be worth a great deal. Winston Churchill's still secret World War II papers would fetch more than their weight in gold. So would the Foreign Office files on the Suez war. They would make an instant best seller for any historian who could get his hands on them.'

'So it was secret papers he was after?' said Robinson.

'*They* were after,' corrected Peter. 'Carrington *and* Thrasher. America is a better market for this sort of thing than Europe. Which is why Thrasher replaced Bodley.'

'Why the long run-up from autumn to winter?' asked Jeremy Whitaker. 'Wouldn't it be simpler to finish the job in a week? In summer, when the coatless ploy wouldn't be needed?'

'The timing is a clue to what actually happened,' replied Peter. 'You know how the press are let loose at the end of the year on papers which have surfaced under the thirty-year rule? By the same token secret papers that won't be released for the *next* thirty years are deposited in the PRO each December. Carrington wanted the latest crop, which had to be lifted in December.'

'He needed time to establish the coatless image?' said Jeremy.

'Exactly. And he'd have got away with it but for Wigmore's blackmail. The two crimes bumped into each other. Carrington got into the stackroom, but Wigmore must have turned up unexpectedly and had to be eliminated. Carrington shoved his body into the paternoster and got down to the job he'd come to do — helping himself to saleable papers. What they were I've no idea, but I bet a search will show that something — something juicy — is missing.'

'How did he get the papers out of the stackroom?' asked Robinson. 'Your theory that if he was caught he would pretend he was looking for the loo wouldn't help much if he had a boxful of top secret papers under his arm.'

'This was the second reason for an accomplice. Having found what he wanted Carrington put the papers in a box the number of which was pre-arranged with Thrasher. Say box ADM (for Admiralty) 199 1234.

'Thrasher turns up on Thursday morning, brings the fictitious Carrington through the turnstile, asks the computer to send ADM 199 1234, waits fifteen minutes for it to arrive, removes the stolen papers, returns the box and then beats it.'

'Which is why he was in such a hurry when we arrived,' said Robinson.

'Ideally he would have left at leisure. It was the murder that sent him on his way so rapidly. With the papers, whatever they are, which will make a fortune in the States.'

'*Not* the States.'

The keeper had returned unobtrusively and had been listening to the later stages of Peter's exposition. He went on:

'You might as well know now. I've just had a call from — well, I needn't say. The short point is that last year's Joint Intelligence Committee papers have just turned up in New York.'

Peter Plumb whistled.

'The JIC papers! You could hardly do better! The nation's secrets bounded in a nutshell. Worth a fortune — but *not* in the States?'

The keeper went on:

'Since most of our secrets are shared with the Americans the value of the JIC papers to them is not great. They were destined for the Russians, to whom their value would be immeasurable.'

'*Destined*?' asked Jeremy Whitaker.

'They never reached them. The CIA have had their eye on Professor Thrasher for some time. By the judicious use of an *agent provocateur* they have recovered the papers, thereby preserving a good many of their own secrets as well as ours. I assume, Inspector, that in the light of this information, and Mr Plumb's statement, you will get a warrant for Mr Carrington's arrest. He is still working in the Reading Room on his monograph on gambling.'

'Don't need a warrant for a murder charge,' replied Robinson. 'Come on, Jim, before the bird flies.'

'Just a sec,' put in Peter Plumb. 'Give us a chance to set up our gear. In the hall outside the Reading Room. We shan't disturb anybody.'

★ ★ ★

'Michael Carrington,' said Inspector Robinson with all the dignity he could muster, being well aware that Peter Plumb's camera was focused on him, in addition to the eyes of the nearby readers, 'I arrest you for the murder of Kevin Wigmore; and I warn you that anything you say may be taken down and used in evidence.'

The readers who heard this formula looked on in grateful astonishment. Many had been present on that memorable occasion when the defunct Wigmore was laid so dramatically at the Princess's feet. On this occasion, however, the principal character in the drama was anything but defunct.

Carrington had no intention of going quietly. He leaped to his feet — almost a reflex action — and instead of rushing from the Reading Room, as might have been expected, bolted through the stack-room door and slammed it behind him with a mighty clang.

Robinson was momentarily taken aback, but soon recovered himself. Remembering there was only one door to the stackroom he cried to Tough:

'We've got him bottled up. Get hold of the key!'

Before Tough could move, the telephone on Ronald Rollem's desk shrilled. The assistant keeper was tempted to ignore it, suspecting that the call was probably from some tiresome citizen wanting to know what part his great-great-grandfather played in the Crimean war, and that if he answered he would miss some part of the drama now being

302

enacted. Loyalty to the taxpayer prevailed and he lifted the receiver.

A moment later he called to the inspector:

'It's him! Calling from the stackroom. Wants to speak to you!'

Robinson took the instrument and listened, his face growing grave. When he hung up he said:

'Trouble! Says he's got enough petrol to set the whole place on fire. Took it in the day of the murder. If we don't believe him, says have a look beneath the stackroom door.'

Tough did so, and returned quickly.

'It's petrol all right. He's spilled some under the door. Sort of sample.'

'Nothing must be done to endanger the archives,' said the keeper. '*Nothing*!'

'All very well,' said Robinson. 'So far as I'm concerned, *everything* must be done to bring a murderer to book.'

'*And* a traitor,' murmured Peter Plumb.

'How serious *is* the fire danger?' asked Robinson.

'The floors and walls are reinforced concrete,' replied the keeper. 'But the records are paper and parchment, dry as tinder. Pile up a few boxes and soak them with petrol — it's unthinkable. Event *without* petrol the whole place is at risk. It will be a tragedy if a single record is lost, a million tragedies if there's a major fire. I must talk to the Lord Chancellor. And you, Inspector, must do nothing to precipitate a crisis until I get instructions.'

'Oh, God!' Robinson muttered to Tough. 'Why didn't I take early retirement when I had the offer?'

'What about the readers?' Pepperbred asked when the keeper had gone. 'And staff?'

'Send them away,' replied the inspector. 'All of them — except staff concerned with fire-fighting. You'd better alert the fire brigade.'

Within fifteen minutes the building was empty except for the keeper, his deputies, Pepperbred, and a group of security officers who doubled as firefighters. Peter Plumb and his crew had the sense to keep in the background, hoping that no-one would try to extend the order to evacuate the building to them.

'I got the Lord Chancellor,' said the keeper on his return to the deserted Reading Room. 'They had to bring him out of a meeting. He's going to raise the SAS. Meantime we do nothing.'

Pepperbred had marshalled the security guards who now stood by the firehoses near the stackroom door. He had explained the situation to the Richmond Fire Brigade who agreed to send all their available appliances and a squad with breathing apparatus. They also warned neighbouring brigades that they might have a major conflagration on their hands before the day was out. There was now nothing for it but to await developments.

The first was another call on Rollem's phone, now manned by Sergeant Tough. 'Carrington?' asked Robinson. Tough nodded and scribbled in his notebook. When he had finished he said, hand over mouthpiece:

'Says he's piled up FO 371 boxes, next to the WO 106 shelves. We're to tell the keeper that unless he's guaranteed safe conduct that lot will go up in smoke.'

'He couldn't have chosen better,' said

the keeper grimly when this news was relayed to him. 'If FO 371 goes it's the end of study of our foreign policy. WO 106 is Military Operations and Intelligence — equally important. To say nothing of the other stuff that may go if the fire catches on. All we can do is keep him talking.'

'He must know he can't get away with it,' said Robinson.

The telephone was speaking again. Tough put the receiver to his ear.

'He says he must have a hostage to cover him while he leaves. He has a gun and won't hesitate to use it if there's any funny business.'

'Tell him,' instructed Robinson, 'we need time to find a volunteer. We'll let him know when we have one.'

'The Lord Chancellor's on his way,' reported the keeper, who had been called to another telephone. 'And a detachment of the SAS. Should be here within an hour. Though what they can do . . . '

'We could starve him out,' suggested Tough.

'If we had a guarantee he wouldn't

start his fire,' said the keeper. 'Think of the damage if he *does* go for the records.' He shuddered. 'It could be the greatest national disaster since the Cotton Library went up in smoke.'

Neither Robinson nor Tough had heard of the Cotton Library, but no doubt the keeper had a point. They prayed for the arrival of the Lord Chancellor and the SAS squad before Carrington carried out his threat.

In the event they arrived simultaneously, the Lord Chancellor in an official car from Westminster, the SAS by helicopter, which landed in the now deserted car-park. The captain in charge reported to the Lord Chancellor and keeper for briefing.

'Christ!' he said. 'It won't be easy.'

He inspected the steel door of the stackroom and sniffed the floor where the smell of petrol lingered. He summed up the situation:

'We can do what he asks — give him a hostage, and play it by ear. We can open the door, using the key, and rush him, which may give him enough time to start a fire. We can blow the door, but that could damage the records. It could even start his fire for him. The choice is yours, gentlemen.'

'Who would be the hostage?' asked the Lord Chancellor.

'One of us, sir. No problem there. We're paid to take risks.'

The telephone rang again. Tough reported:

'He's getting impatient. Wants a decision one way or the other.'

'Ask him how long we can have,' said Robinson.

Tough put the question.

'He says fifteen minutes. No more.'

'Well, gentlemen?' said the SAS captain.

'What do you advise?' asked the Lord Chancellor.

'I'd blow the door. Surprise is important. If he's standing near it the explosion may knock him out. We'll take in hand extinguishers, just in case.'

'You'll be careful of the records,' said the keeper anxiously.

'No more foam than is necessary,' said

the SAS man cheerfully.

'Well, Keeper?' said the Lord Chancellor. 'Are we agreed?'

The keeper nodded.

'Inspector?'

'It's out of our hands now,' said Robinson. 'But I've no better plan.'

'OK,' said the SAS captain. 'Everybody to the far end of the room. Except the man on the phone. Sergeant Tough? Right. When I give the signal call him and say we agree about the hostage. He'll be just outside the door. That will put him where we want him.'

The SAS team unloaded their equipment and attached limpets with short fuses to the four corners of the door. Tough recognized them as 'beehives' designed to go through an obstacle rather than to explode into empty space.

When all was ready the captain raised his hand. Tough asked the switchboard to connect him with the stackroom and said:

'Hostage has been agreed. Standing outside the stackroom. You're free to open the door.'

He gave a thumbs-up sign to the

captain, who waited for a moment to give Carrington time to get to the other side of the door and then signalled to his men.

The explosions were deafening. The heavy metal door seemed to crumple and disappear into the stackroom. Three SAS men followed it through a dense cloud of smoke.

There came an anguished groan from the keeper, crouched behind a table, wondering what damage had been done, and what more might be done, to the nation's archives. He hurried across to the scene of destruction closely followed by the others. Peter Plumb rubbed his hands with glee. There is nothing a TV audience enjoys more than a good explosion.

It was some time before the smoke cleared. When it did there was no sign of Carrington. He would hardly have disintegrated even had he been standing behind the door, but for a moment it seemed to be the only explanation. There was no sign of a pile of combustible records, nor of petrol cans full or empty. Then one of the SAS men saw a small tin near the remains of the door — of lighter fuel. He held it up.

'Petrol my Aunt Fanny!' he said. 'We've been had! He poured some lighter fuel under the door to make us think he could start a fire.'

'Where is he?' demanded the keeper, overjoyed that the records seemed to be intact. 'He must be somewhere. And he said he's armed.'

'Bluffing,' said the SAS captain. 'The petrol was a bluff and the gun's a bluff too. Stay here while we look around.'

The team dispersed through the stackroom, Stens at the ready. There was no sign of anybody. Peter, who with his crew had approached to get a close-up of the wrecked door, had a sudden inspiration.

'Come on, chaps!' he yelled.

He led them to the terminus of the paternoster and motioned the cameraman to focus on its door. Already he detected the rumble of machinery heralding the arrival of a paternoster wagon. He knew it would not carry the great map of Calais or any other outsize document; and he was not disappointed. The coffinlike container which nosed its way into the Reading Room was bearing Michael Carrington to freedom; or it would have done had not Peter Plumb and Jeremy Whitaker fallen upon him before he could rise from his bizarre chariot.

20

At its first showing Peter Plumb's masterpiece drew the largest audience ever to view a TV documentary in Britain. The film found itself high in the top ten of all programmes. Jeremy Whitaker invited a select group to his Barnes home to celebrate the event, including Peter and his camera crew, the film editor and other technicians, and senior officials from the Public Record Office. Inspector Robinson and Sergeant Tough were also present. They'd seen a preview of the film and were more than satisfied that justice had been done to their contribution.

When the credits finally disappeared, champagne glasses were refilled and a wave of general congratulation followed.

Peter resisted demands for a formal speech but said:

'D'ye realize how touch and go it was? I mean our nabbing Carrington? With a bit of luck he'd have got away. He guessed everybody would rush into the stackroom and that by coming out through the paternoster he'd have a clear field. The building had been evacuated so there was nobody to stop him. If I hadn't had the bright idea — '

'There's no need to boast,' said Jeremy Whitaker, as he wandered round the room filling glasses. 'Simply because your criminal mind thought along the same lines as his. What's more, you'd better get it into your head that when somebody hardly out of his Pampers does something like this the future is bleak.'

'Meaning?'

Peter was now floating happily on euphoric clouds of success and champagne, impervious to anything his superior might have to say, tongue in cheek, or straight from the heart.

'There's only one way you can go now. Down.'

'Aren't you being rather hard, Mr Whitaker?' said the keeper.

He was already wondering what the consequences would be for the PRO.

How would it cope with the huge number of viewers likely to visit it as a result of the documentary?

'We're really proud of the boy,' confessed Jeremy. 'But we mustn't allow it to go to his head. More champagne, Keeper?'

★   ★   ★

The trial of Michael Carrington at the Old Bailey had ended two weeks earlier with a stinging summing-up by the judge in which he admitted it was difficult to decide which was the more shameful: the cold-blooded murder of Kevin Wigmore, admittedly a blackmailer, but so far as Carrington was concerned an innocent citizen, or the attempt to sell secrets vital to the security of the nation to a hostile power.

It would seem that in the event he decided that they were equally reprehensible, for he sentenced the former SIS man to twenty-five years for the murder and another twenty-five for his treasonable activities, the two sentences to run consecutively.

The judge also had some harsh things to say about Carrington's ruthless attempt to involve his friend Richard Bodley in his nefarious activities, by seeking to bankrupt him. It had now been definitely established that the removal of Bodley's household effects had been engineered by Carrington to make his friend an accomplice; and when a more useful accomplice had presented himself in the shape of Hiram Thrasher — who was now facing charges of espionage in the United States — Carrington had no compunction in throwing his friend overboard.

As for Bodley he could hardly believe the risks he had been running. He calculated that when Carrington was eventually released he would have reached the ripe old age of approximately one hundred and ten; and he shuddered to think that he, Bodley, might easily have suffered the same fate.

One consequence of these events was that he awarded himself a life sentence. Although the idea of matrimony had never occurred either to him or to

Ernestine Dudley before they met each other, during their association in the Public Record Office it did, and steadily matured. To his enormous astonishment Bodley asked her to marry him. To her even greater astonishment she accepted.

★ ★ ★

Alistair Macalister, freed from a murder charge by the arrest and subsequent conviction of Carrington, still had to answer for the theft of public documents. After lengthy consideration the Director of Public Prosecutions decided that no punishment could exceed the withdrawal of his right to study in the Public Record Office, which together with the attendant disgrace would effectively end his career as a historian. In various press interviews he made a great deal of this. He painted a grim picture of his penurious future which drew much sympathy from those who saw his only crime as the theft of a few mouldy old papers of no value to anyone.

The inner cabinet of Megalith Industries were faced by a secret they would have to take to their graves. The only way to prevent the kidnapping from being seen as a conspiracy with dire consequences was to keep silent about it, and to ensure Macalister's silence also.

Sir Maurice Dyer said:

'We've no choice. Macalister saved our bacon by burning the memorandum.'

'We let the deal stand?' said Gilbert Archer. 'He collects the half million?'

'We could beat him down,' suggested Bernard Mitchell. 'Settle for say fifty thousand?'

'Aren't we playing with fire to change the arrangements?' said Dyer. 'The bank assumes that a half million ransom was paid. Can we suddenly return it and expect no awkward questions?'

'No,' said Archer with decision. 'The matter's closed. We paid half a million to safeguard the missile contract. It was a small price. Now that the contract's in the bag I've no doubt the shareholders will applaud our humanitarian attitude in rescuing our chairman. And so they should.'

'So we let him have the money — and forget the whole thing.'

'Agreed.'

'That hateful young man gets away with it?'

'No alternative, Maurice. It's said that when the law fails to mete out the appropriate punishment crime brings its own punishment, usually much more severe.'

'That may be true in the realms of fiction, Gilbert. Virtue always triumphs. Vice, never. But in this case . . . It doesn't bear thinking of.'

'Forget it, Maurice. Let's go up to lunch, there's something special on the menu to celebrate the missile contract — and the rosy future of MIL.'

MURDER IN DUPLICATE

Peter Conway

When Jennifer Prentice, a student nurse, was found dead in a locked bathroom, Inspector Newton went to St. Aldhelm's Hospital to investigate . . . Newton finds the Matron, Miss Diana Digby Scott, unapproachable. Why was Alison Carter so disliked by Jennifer? Is Vernon Pritchard, the surgeon who was having an affair with Jennifer, telling the truth? Before Newton finds any answers, there is another death and he faces mortal danger himself.

A QUESTION OF MURDER

R. H. Lees

When Arthur Burnett died in the Rhodesian bush, Randall realised that Burnett was the one mentioned in the cryptogram. Inspector Sturman ridiculed Randall's suggestion that it could be foul play. So Randall proves that one of Burnett's African employees had been murdered and finds a mystic hill which only one African would dare to climb . . . Whilst observing animal behaviour, he comes upon a gruesome scene and almost loses his own life before solving the mystery.